"How about plan B?"

Drew continued, "My brothers have their own places on the ranch. It's just my grandfather and me at the big house. I can easily move you and Mae into your own rooms."

"Oh, I don't know," Sadie fairly groaned. She liked living alone, and there was comfort in her routine. What Drew proposed sounded chaotic to her, even if it was only for the weekend.

He shrugged as though reading her thoughts. "Your other option is the local inn. We can move Mae's bed and all there."

"What?" Sadie straightened. "Wait a minute. For the moment, we're both guardians. That means you, too."

"Yep. That's why the ranch is the perfect solution."

The ranch is a terrible solution. "Fine," she muttered. "The ranch it is."

Drew chuckled. "That's the spirit."

Sadie resisted the urge to roll her eyes like her students did.

Her life had been turned on its head, and she'd just agreed to live with two men and a baby. She took a deep breath. What else could possibly go wrong?

Tina Radcliffe has been dreaming and scribbling for years. Originally from Western New York, she left home for a tour of duty with the US Army Security Agency stationed in Augsburg, Germany, and ended up in Tulsa, Oklahoma. Her past careers include certified oncology RN, library cataloger and pharmacy clerk. She recently moved from Denver, Colorado, to the Phoenix, Arizona, area, where she writes heartwarming and fun inspirational romance.

Books by Tina Radcliffe

Love Inspired Suspense

Sabotaged Mission

Love Inspired

Lazy M Ranch

The Baby Inheritance

Hearts of Oklahoma

Finding the Road Home
Ready to Trust
His Holiday Prayer
The Cowgirl's Sacrifice

Visit the Author Profile page
at LoveInspired.com for more titles.

The Baby Inheritance

Tina Radcliffe

LOVE INSPIRED
INSPIRATIONAL ROMANCE

LOVE INSPIRED®
INSPIRATIONAL ROMANCE

Recycling programs
for this product may
not exist in your area.

ISBN-13: 978-1-335-58569-1

The Baby Inheritance

Copyright © 2023 by Tina M. Radcliffe

For questions and comments about the quality of this book, please contact us
at CustomerService@Harlequin.com.

Love Inspired
22 Adelaide St. West, 41st Floor
Toronto, Ontario M5H 4E3, Canada
www.LoveInspired.com

Printed in U.S.A.

But this one thing I do, forgetting those things
which are behind, and reaching forth
unto those things which are before.
—*Philippians* 3:13

The Lazy M Ranch series evolved from a single note card sent to me by fellow writer Deborah Clack. The card depicted the silhouette of six cowboys standing together in the shadows facing a corral. The photography on that card is by Sherry Peters of BradburyLane.com. Sherry is a lovely woman of God who sent me the full-size print of the original card. It now hangs in my office. Thank you, Deborah and Sherry, for your hand in creating *The Baby Inheritance*.

Additional inspirational credit goes to my fabulous Wrangler Team, especially Nicole C, Kim Ann, Cindy W and Kimberly B, who named various characters and events in this series.

A big thank-you to my cousin Mary Ellen Colangelo for the ricotta cookie recipe.

I'm also sending thanks to Josee Telfer, a constant encourager.

Finally, thank you to my discerning editor Katie Gowrie and my wonderful agent, Jessica Alvarez, who made this series a reality. I am honored to be on this journey with these amazing women in my corner.

Chapter One

Drew Morgan wiped the sweat from his brow and leaned against the barn door.

In front of him, nimbostratus clouds stretched long gray fingers across the Oklahoma sky, promising that rain was on the way.

One o'clock in the afternoon, and he'd already put in a day's work.

The first calves of the season had birthed this morning, and while that gave him a deep sense of satisfaction, the tragic irony of the circle of life hadn't escaped him.

Only five months ago, he'd attended the funeral of his friends. Jase and Delia Franklin. Young parents—gone too soon, courtesy of a drunk driver. Now it was already late March, and newborn calves, budding trees and foliage all indicated time was moving on.

The vibration of his cell phone pulled Drew from his musing. He eased the device from the back pocket of his Wranglers and answered without checking the caller ID.

"Lazy M Ranch. Drew Morgan."

"Drew." His grandfather's scratchy baritone greeted him. "You missed lunch."

"I'm almost done here."

"You've been working yourself ragged for months."

"I know, Gramps," Drew murmured. Yeah, he knew, but hard work delivered the balm of distraction. He couldn't think about the loss of his friends and pound a fence post at the same time.

His grandfather released a breath that told Drew he was shaking his head. "Well, you got a phone call at the house. That lawyer's office in town. The secretary says you're due there about now."

Drew blinked. He had completely forgotten the appointment.

"You got an issue needing a lawyer, son?"

"Not to my knowledge." Drew didn't have a clue as to why he'd been summoned to the attorney's office. He'd received the letter a week ago and promptly ignored the missive, figuring it probably wasn't good news.

"Well, you better hustle," Gramps continued.

Hustle was right. There was no time to change or shower. The red Oklahoma clay had barely dried on his boots by the time he'd jumped into his dually and arrived in downtown Homestead Pass.

Drew dusted off his Wranglers and work shirt as best he could then opened the door to the attorney's office. Helen Franklin, Jase's mother, looked up from her seat in the waiting room and smiled. Was he imagining the pallor of her skin and the frail appearance?

Helen held a blue-eyed, smiling baby on her lap. Jase and Delia's baby. The pudgy dimpled cheeks and golden curls of the six-month-old tripped Drew's heartstrings.

Next to Helen sat Sadie Ross, Delia's best friend. The college professor wore a charcoal-gray business suit, and her ebony hair was tied up in a twist at the back of her head. He noted the stylish burgundy heels with little bows on her feet—a contrast to her otherwise prim demeanor.

Sadie seemed as surprised to see him as he was to see her.

Drew cringed when her brown eyes assessed his mud-spattered clothing.

Before the funeral, his last memory of Sadie was at Jase and Delia's wedding. She'd been maid of honor to Drew's best man. The wedding had paired off the two most incompatible people on the planet. It wasn't that he didn't like the woman. He plain didn't get her. Sadie was literal and tightly wound. A far cry from his laid-back nature.

"Helen, good to see you," Drew finally said. He turned to Sadie again and offered a nod of greeting as realization dawned.

Today's appointment is about Jase and Delia.

"Good to see you as well, Drew," Helen said. "Keeping busy at the ranch?"

"Yes, ma'am. Spring calving."

The oak door to the office of Mason Whitaker, attorney-at-law, opened. Dread fought to gain a foothold within Drew, but he pushed it away. Once they were all seated inside, the lawyer handed out official-looking papers to Drew and Sadie.

"Mrs. Franklin and I reviewed the terms of Jason and Delia Franklin's will months ago. However, a situation has come up that demands we review it again, with both of you."

Drew longed to ask the obvious question but remained silent, allowing the slow-talking attorney to get to the point.

"Most of the will is standard. In accordance with their wishes, the bulk of the estate has been left to Mrs. Helen Franklin, mother of the deceased, Jason Franklin. The life insurance benefits have been designated for the minor, Mae Anne Franklin. The funds are for her needs now, and additionally, an education trust fund is available when she turns eighteen for college expenses."

Drew listened carefully, still trying to understand why he was here. He glanced at Sadie, and she, too, seemed perplexed.

"Currently, Mrs. Franklin has custody of Mae." The attorney looked at Jase's mother. "Would you like to share the rest?"

"You're doing just fine, son."

"All right, then." He nodded. "Mrs. Franklin—"

"Helen. These kids know me as Helen."

"Helen has recently been diagnosed with, ah…a significant medical challenge. She's scheduled to have surgery next week at St. Francis Hospital in Tulsa."

Startled by the information, Drew found his mouth dry, without an appropriate response. While he searched for words, Sadie turned to Helen.

"Oh, my," she said. "I'll certainly be praying."

Helen patted Sadie's hand. "I'd appreciate that, dear."

The attorney cleared his throat, and all eyes focused on him again. "Due to an anticipated rigorous treatment schedule, following surgery, Helen finds it necessary to relinquish custody of Mae."

What? Before Drew could process the information, Whitaker continued.

"If you'll turn to page ten, section four."

Pages rustled. Drew's gaze zeroed in on the section mentioned, and he froze at the sight of his name.

"Before their untimely deaths, Jason and Delia designated both of you as their choice for guardians for Mae Anne Franklin if the situation warranted. Per the state of Oklahoma laws, as the designated guardians are not married, one of you will be named the permanent primary guardian."

Guardian? Sure, he remembered being honored when Jase had asked him to be a godparent to his child. Never in his wildest dreams did he imagine this day would come.

Sadie's face had paled, revealing that she was also stunned.

A ringtone trilled, and Helen reached into her purse to pull out a cell phone. "Oh, dear. It's my oncologist's office. Will you excuse me?" She stood with the baby in her arms and smiled at Sadie. "Would you mind taking Mae?"

"I, um… Okay."

At the handoff, Sadie awkwardly cradled the pink bundle on her lap, looking for all the world as though she'd never held a baby before.

Sensing her panic, Drew reached over and easily scooped up Mae. "I've got her," he murmured. Once in his arms, Mae began to chatter, babbling vowels and consonants like a conversation.

"Thank you," Sadie mumbled.

Drew offered a nod and turned to the attorney. "What exactly does guardianship mean?"

"It will require a background check, paperwork and a legal proceeding." He paused and leaned forward, lowering his voice. "I'm going to give it to you two off the record. As you are aware, Helen was a late-life mother. Now, at seventy-eight and widowed, she's taken over the care of her only grandchild. That alone is amazing. But her health is failing, and her prognosis is not hopeful." He glanced between them, his eyes reflecting the seriousness of the situation.

"Though you are not obligated, keep in mind that if neither of you is willing to assume guardianship and because there are no other relatives, Mae could be turned over to the Department of Human Services for temporary foster placement."

Sadie gasped. "Foster care?" She stiffened and gave an adamant shake of her head. "No. That's not happening. Delia and I met in foster care. I know that she would never want that."

"So, you agree to guardianship?" the attorney persisted.

"I don't see how there can be any other choice," Sadie returned. "Yes. I absolutely agree."

"Whoa. Just a minute," Drew said. He glanced down at Mae, who wriggled on his lap, bright-eyed and oblivious to the fact that her future was on the line. This was his best buddy's child and an obligation that he couldn't, wouldn't, ignore. "Let's not move too fast. I'm interested as well."

Sadie shot him a surprised expression. "I live and work in Tulsa. That's where Helen is receiving treatment. It makes sense for me to take over the care of Mae."

"Homestead Pass is where Jase and Delia chose to raise their child. It's where Helen lives." He released a sound of frustration. "Tulsa's three hours from here, Sadie."

"Perhaps I should give you two time to discuss this," the attorney said. As he spoke, the door to his office opened, and Helen stepped back into the room.

"I'm sorry about that." The older woman glanced between Drew and Sadie and frowned. "Is everything all right?"

"Oh, yeah," Drew said. "It's all good. We're chatting about the logistics."

"I see." Helen nodded slowly. "I know I've put both of you in a difficult situation, but please know that I've prayed long and hard. Mae has already had such an upheaval in her life. I need to know that she's settled in a happy home with someone who will welcome my grandmotherly doting when I'm able." She swiped the trail of moisture that had spilled from her eyes. "I hate leaving my little sweetheart. But I have consolation knowing that Jase and Delia trusted you two."

"Don't worry, Helen," Drew said. "We'll figure this out."

Sadie looked at him, her expression clearly questioning his claim.

"I start treatment on Monday, so I'm hoping Mae can get settled with one of you today."

"Today?" Sadie squeaked out the word, which mirrored his thoughts.

"I'll be only a phone call away," Helen said. "I'm staying with a friend in Tulsa during treatments. In between, I'll be back in Homestead Pass."

Drew gave a slow, confident nod as though everything was going to work out fine. Inside, a dozen questions pummeled him.

"And I can assure you, Mae is a delightful child," Helen continued. "She sleeps through the night and hardly ever fusses. I've brought along Delia's notebook detailing her schedule, foods of preference, and pertinent medical information."

"Medical?" Drew frowned. Jase hadn't mentioned any health issues.

"Oh, no worries. She's very healthy," Helen assured. "No allergies. The pediatrician is monitoring her for a minor issue that is expected to resolve itself. She's got a check-up with a specialist next week, which I'll send the details for."

Helen pulled out an enormous three-ring binder and handed it to Sadie.

"Delia did this?" Sadie peeked inside at the typed and tabbed notebook before she placed the hefty tome on the floor between them.

"That's an impressive binder," Drew said.

"Yes. Quite comprehensive," Helen said. "And here are

the keys to Jase and Delia's house. I've been staying there with Mae, but last weekend I moved back to my place."

An ache settled in Drew's chest as he took the keys. Delia and Jase had built the home located on the outskirts of Homestead Pass with plans to raise their family in the country.

"Though it breaks my heart, I'll be selling their house soon," Helen said. "The realty office in Homestead Pass says the market will peak in the summer with the influx of tourists." She paused. "If it will help with the transition, we can keep the place until you have a plan."

"A plan…" Drew murmured. Yeah, a plan was exactly what they needed right now.

Thirty minutes later it was all over, and Drew and Sadie stood outside the law office on the sidewalk. Mae's diaper bag and car seat sat on the ground beside them as they faced off awkwardly. Vehicles moved past them down Main Street. Business as usual for a Thursday afternoon in late March. Except it wasn't. Not at all.

"What just happened?" Sadie murmured.

"You tell me." Drew shook his head. "If I understand correctly, we'll meet back at the attorney's office once Helen returns from Tulsa, to start the paperwork for guardianship. We have until then to decide which of us will be the primary caregiver."

"That's what I thought he said. Not we, but one of us. One of us will be signing the paperwork."

"Yep." He nodded. "You have a lot of experience with babies?"

Sadie stared at the bows on her shiny heels. "None."

"None? Then why did you volunteer for guardianship?" Drew cocked his head, trying to read between the lines. Did the woman understand what she'd signed up for?

"I wanted the option of foster care off the table," she

shot back, eyes bright. "What about you? Why did you volunteer?"

That was a good question with a complicated answer. Was it because Jase had been like another brother? A lifetime of friendship ought to mean something. Or maybe because in thirty-odd years, this was the first hard thing his friend had ever asked him to do.

Drew shrugged. "It was the right thing to do."

The right thing? Was the right thing the best thing for Mae? He didn't know the answer, and the question continued to gnaw at him.

Around them, the sky seemed to darken, and the wind kicked up. A scrap of paper danced past and continued down Main Street.

"Where are you staying?" Drew adjusted Mae in his arms and pulled up the hood of her pink jacket.

"Homestead Pass Inn. I took off today and Friday, thinking I'd head back to Tulsa on Sunday," Sadie said. "I'm due in class on Monday."

"I guess you think this will be resolved by then."

"That's not it at all," she sputtered. "I had no idea this was going to happen." Her eyes rounded, bright with indignation. "Did you?"

"Nope. I came here straight from the barn. I'm as surprised as you are." Mae's little lips rounded with almost words that had both him and Sadie looking at the cheerful six-month-old.

Sadie lifted her head and met his gaze. He recognized the pain and confusion in her brown eyes as reflecting his own.

"What are we going to do?" she asked. Despair laced her voice as the question burst from her lips.

"I don't have a clue." Drew ducked farther beneath the awning of the attorney's office as rain began to spit.

"Maybe we should start by picking up Mae's supplies at… the house."

"Okay." She sounded numb. As though she'd take any refuge from the confusion of the sad circumstances that brought them together.

"Mind if we take my truck?"

"Sure. My car's a very small hybrid."

Minutes later, Sadie and Drew sat silently in his pickup with Mae safely strapped into her car seat in the back seat of the extended cab. Outside, the sky had opened and rain pounded the truck. Drops furiously tap-danced on the windshield.

Drew stared out at the blurry gray scenery. "I'll head out when this rain eases up," he said.

Sadie nodded and released a long sigh.

He glanced over at the passenger seat, where the professor inched closer to the window, adjusting her polished high heels to avoid a discarded rag on the floorboard.

Weren't they a pair? The only thing the two of them had in common was Sadie's question that played in his mind on a constant loop.

What are we going to do?

He'd figured someday he'd have a family of his own. A happy marriage like his parents and maybe a couple of kids too. Though when he'd turned forty last month, he'd begun to suspect that might never happen. Now here he was, sitting in a truck with the woman least likely to fulfill any of his aspirations of happily ever after and a sweet baby who needed parents.

The good Lord was in charge.

Yet, this was not exactly how he'd imagined the next chapter of his life would kick off.

Sadie waited on the porch of Jase and Delia's house while Drew unlocked the door and disarmed the security system per Helen Franklin's written instructions. She glanced down at Mae, sleeping in the car seat carrier. The baby's pink bow-shaped mouth curved into a smile in slumber. Not a care in the world.

Little Mae could teach her a thing or two, it seemed. Casting her cares upon the Lord remained a perpetual struggle for Sadie.

She paced the length of the porch while she waited, her heels clicking on the wooden planks. The pale yellow house sat on an acre of land outside the small town of Homestead Pass, with a view of tall conifers that surrounded a small pond. Large navy glazed pots sat on either side of the cobblestone walkway, waiting for Delia to plant blooms in them once the last frost passed.

A sigh was all Sadie could muster as a dark chasm of grief consumed her. She didn't dare release her bottled-up emotions, or she might never stop crying. Besides, experience had taught her that tears never solved anything.

"I forgot what a big house this is," Drew said as he held the door open.

Sadie gripped the carrier handle and stepped over the threshold with Mae. Her gaze took in the vaulted ceiling and white walls. Yes, it was a big house, but Delia had said they would fill it to the rafters with kids. Her lips trembled at the thought.

"Who cleans a place this size?" Drew glanced down at his boots and balanced on one foot at a time to remove them before treading farther into the house.

"Delia had a housekeeper," Sadie said.

"I don't suppose she had a nanny as well?"

"No. Delia was hands-on all the way." Sadie gently placed the carrier on the plush gray carpet and walked around the spacious living room. Closing her eyes briefly, she recalled the last time she'd been here. Delia sat on the couch with Jase perched on the arm as they smiled down at their new baby. They were so much in love. So much in love with their child, their life.

"What do you think about staying here?" Drew asked.

Sadie whirled around, aghast. "Me?"

"Yeah. You and Mae. Cheaper than the inn and everything you'd need."

"Oh, no. No. No. You cannot leave me with a baby. Don't even think about it."

"Easy." He raised his palms in defense. "You were the one who jumped at guardianship."

"Yes. I did. The truth is, I sort of freaked out when that lawyer mentioned foster care. Delia was the only family I've ever had. That makes Mae family too." She met his gaze. "Does that make sense?"

"Sure, it does. I couldn't have said it better. Jase was family, and that makes Mae family."

Sadie stared into his pale blue eyes and saw understanding. At that moment, a bit of her tension slipped away.

"Unfortunately," she continued, "that doesn't mean I know how to care for a baby." Once again, her gaze scanned the room. "And this house. This house is much too painful. The memories…" Head reeling, a rush of heat warmed her face and she eased into a chair.

"You okay?" Drew asked.

"Yes, I'm fine." Sadie ran her fingers over the nubby fabric of the chair's arm. She would be fine, eventually.

The sounds of Mae fussing in the carrier filled the stretch of silence, and Drew wasted no time freeing the baby from the contraption. He unzipped the pink jacket and eased it from her tiny body. Only moments later, Mae sat in Drew's arms, her back against his chest, looking out at the world.

How did he do that so easily? She longed to be the maternal type, like Delia, but somehow that gene seemed to have passed her by.

"You're very good with babies," Sadie said. "Do you have children?" The question popped from her mouth before she had time to yank it back in.

He grinned as though amused at the question. "No children."

"I don't mean to be intrusive." She backtracked quickly.

"I hear a *but*," Drew said.

"Well, it suddenly occurred to me that I don't know much about you, except that you have a ranch and you're Jase's best friend."

"I'm an open book. Nothing in my closet except old boots." He smiled. "I majored in architectural engineering at Oklahoma State University. I run the Lazy M Ranch with my three brothers and my grandfather."

Sadie nodded. Architecture? That surprised her. What was he doing on a ranch? And she couldn't help but notice that his answer didn't extend to whether he'd been married or had a steady girlfriend. She assumed women were knocking down his door. Why wouldn't they? He was an intelligent guy. Not to mention tall and good-looking, with that unruly caramel-colored hair. Plus, he had a promising future. But there was no way she would actually ask him. The response might bring even more complications to their tricky situation.

"How about you?" He cocked his head in question. "I mean, since we are coparenting for the weekend, at least. Do you have a fella back in Tulsa?"

Sadie's eyes widened. Of course he'd ask the question she'd shied away from.

"I'm not in a relationship. If that's what you mean."

At her words, baby Mae began to fuss in earnest, releasing a plaintive cry as her arms flailed against Drew's chest.

"Now what?" Sadie asked, her anxiety rising in direct proportion to Mae's screams.

He glanced at his watch. "She's likely hungry. Helen said she put a prepared bottle in the bag. Mind fetching it?"

Sadie scrambled to the diaper bag and searched the pockets then the main compartment. Diapers, blankets, toys, pacifiers, wet wipes and more. This baby had more supplies than Sadie had packed for her trip to Homestead Pass. "I don't see a bottle in here."

"Look for an insulated container."

She continued to search. Hands shaking, Sadie finally pulled the bottle from the depths of the bag. "Aha!"

"Want to warm it up for me?"

For a split second, Sadie stared at him. She could recite Shakespearean sonnets and offer random trivia about the Elizabethan period, but she didn't have any idea how to warm a baby bottle.

"Warm. It. Up?" she finally said. "I don't know how to do that."

He thrust Mae into her arms and took the bottle. "Okay, you watch Mae. I've got this."

"Watch Mae. Right." Sadie followed him into the kitchen with her arms clasping the baby around the middle. There was no way she'd drop Delia's child.

Heels clicking on the tiled floor, she hurried to catch up with Drew's long strides, jostling Mae in the process. But the more Sadie moved, the more Mae calmed down. So, she continued moving around the huge kitchen. Back and forth in front of the granite-topped island.

Both Sadie and Mae focused on Drew's every move as he opened and closed cupboards.

He found a deep bowl, filled it with water and put it in the microwave. Then he pulled the bowl out and checked the water temperature with his fingers before placing the bottle in the water.

"The key is to warm, not cook, the milk." He swirled the bottle in the liquid, then removed and gently inverted it a few times. "Then test the temperature of the milk on the wrist."

Sadie mentally repeated the steps. If only she had her laptop. She'd never remember all the steps unless she wrote them down to study later.

Drew easily slipped Mae from Sadie's arms, popped off the nipple cover and offered the bottle. Enthused, the baby latched immediately, her little hands holding the bottle in place like a pro.

Sadie could only stare, amazed. "If you don't have children, how do you know how to do that?"

He raised his shoulders in a slow shrug. "I don't know. My brothers Trevor and Lucas were born when I was a kid. I used to watch my mother. Besides, it's the same principle as bottle-feeding a calf. Right?"

"Uh, right." A baby and a calf were both foreign entities in her world.

For minutes they both silently observed as Mae finished the bottle.

"So now you burp her," Sadie said. She did know the rudimentary steps from television and movies.

"Unless she burps first. Then we'll change her diaper."

We? Sadie cringed, unable to hide her dismay.

Drew chuckled. "You've got that look on your face again."

"Of course I do. I have never changed a diaper either. Have you?"

"No. But I think the secret here is to fake it." He paused. "I'll do it…this time."

"Thank you," she breathed.

Before Drew could change his mind, Sadie escaped the kitchen to wander around the house. She examined the framed life of her friends displayed on a baby grand piano. This house was Delia—and Sadie fully expected to wake from this nightmare and have her friend appear at any moment with her trademark smile and optimism.

But it was Drew who appeared at her side minutes later. She didn't hear him approach, but she sensed him, and her nose picked up on the scent of baby formula and man.

Sadie turned from the array of pictures on the piano to face him. "Where's Mae?"

"I put her in her crib for a bit so we can talk."

Talk? Unless he had a solution to their problem, there wasn't anything to talk about.

"Look, you and I have nothing in common. I get that," Drew continued, his words calm and gentle. "However, we both agree that we don't want Mae in foster care and that she deserves the best future we can promise her."

Sadie nodded and clamped her lips together, once again pushing back a flood of emotions. This situation they found themselves wading into wasn't supposed to happen.

As if sensing her internal battle, Drew became silent. He took a seat on the sofa and balanced his elbows on his knees, hands clasped together. After a few minutes, he cleared his throat. "Were you serious about becoming Mae's guardian?"

"Were you?"

"Yeah, if that attorney is asking."

Confused, Sadie paced back and forth. Then she stopped and met his gaze. "Our best friends are gone, and they entrusted us with their child." She released a long sigh. "The most important thing in Delia and Jase's world."

Drew nodded and studied his hands for a moment. When he looked up, his eyes, fringed by dark lashes, reflected concern. "Yeah. I get that," he said. "The problem is, neither of us is qualified for the job."

Sadie released a sigh. He was partly correct. She wasn't qualified. Not yet, at least. All she needed was a little time and some training. It had been her experience that you could learn anything and everything from a book. Though how she'd manage to balance her busy career and a baby, she didn't know.

Time. That was going to be the real issue here.

"This is getting us nowhere," Drew said. "How about plan B for now? My brothers have their own places on the ranch. It's just my grandfather and me at the big house. I can easily move you and Mae into your own rooms."

"Oh, I don't know," Sadie fairly groaned. She liked living alone, and there was comfort in her routine. What Drew proposed sounded chaotic to her, even if it was only for the weekend.

He shrugged as though reading her thoughts. "Your other option is the inn. We can move Mae's bed and all there."

"What?" Sadie straightened and blinked, processing his words. "Wait a minute. For the moment, we're both guardians. That means you too."

"Yep. That's why the ranch is the perfect solution."

The ranch was a terrible solution, but the best of all the terrible solutions so far.

"Fine," she muttered. "The ranch it is."

Drew chuckled. "That's the spirit."

Sadie resisted the urge to roll her eyes like her students so often did.

Her life had been turned on its head, and she'd just agreed to live with two men and a baby. Sadie took a deep breath. What else could possibly go wrong?

Chapter Two

Once Drew turned into the ranch drive, force of habit had him slowing down. It was a ritual he'd started the day he returned from burying his parents.

Slow down.

Look around.

Be grateful for all the Lord has given you.

A mantra passed on from his father. So, he did, and he was.

Sadie sat silently in the passenger seat, her eyes wide with curiosity as she took in the view past the tall moss-covered stone pillars that stood like sentries beneath the wooden entrance sign.

Drew took pride in the knowledge that his father had built those pillars from local stone and handcrafted the sign with the Lazy M symbol branded into the pine.

Once upon a time, he thought he'd leave all this and see the world, then pursue his dream of becoming an architect. But that was all it was—a dream. The death of his parents right before college graduation had taught him what was important.

Family. Family was everything. Another reason he wanted to be considered for Mae's permanent guardian.

He might not have all the skills needed for the position, but he could offer her family. Lots of family.

The rain had stopped entirely now, and Drew couldn't help but smile when the Morgan homestead came into view. It was a big old rambling jigsaw puzzle of a white clapboard house that had been added on to twice to accommodate the Morgan boys. Despite its imperfections, Drew had a soft spot for the place. Most likely because of the love tucked into the walls.

"I like your house," Sadie said. "It has character."

"Thanks." Drew snuck a peek at Sadie and then eyed the house again. She was right. It did have character, and he found himself impressed and a bit surprised by the comment. He'd figured her tastes ran to urban chic, not down-home country.

Drew pulled the truck close to the porch and put the vehicle in gear with the engine idling, the heater on. In the back seat, Mae stirred briefly and then continued to doze. "Do you mind waiting in the truck while I go to see if anyone is home?" he asked.

He hadn't called his grandfather to prepare him for what was about to descend upon the Lazy M Ranch. Sometimes it was easier to push through than deal with the inevitable twenty questions that Gramps would ask.

"Of course not." She paused. "I hope this isn't going to be an inconvenience." Her lips tightened, and she frowned.

After only a handful of hours with Sadie, already he'd come to recognize her fret-face. Funny, he'd never noticed it at the wedding. Then again, there hadn't been much to be concerned about at that happy event.

"My grandfather will be over the moon to have a baby under the roof. I'll have to tamp down his enthusiasm." Along with any conclusions Gramps would no doubt rush to because Drew had invited Sadie to their home. He'd never brought a woman home with him before, no less a woman and a baby. Gramps would have a good time with that information, though hopefully only Bess, the family housekeeper, was home this time of day.

He exited the truck, took the porch steps two at a time and patted Oliver, the ginger cat sleeping on the porch swing. "Getting your twenty hours of beauty sleep in, pal?" Then he pulled open the screen and the inside door.

"Anyone home?" His boots echoed on the pine floor of the foyer.

"In the kitchen," his grandfather called out.

The aroma of cinnamon urged Drew down the hall and into the spacious farmhouse kitchen, where Gramps sat at the round pedestal table, peeling potatoes. A brown Stetson was perched on the back of his thick, wavy caramel-colored hair. The fact that his grandfather looked like a man at least ten years younger than his actual age never ceased to amaze Drew.

At the sink, the ranch cook and housekeeper of nearly twenty years, Bess Lowder, stood with her hands in soapy water. She turned her head at his entrance, and a welcoming smile split her round face.

"How'd it go with the lawyer?" Gramps asked.

"Hard to explain," Drew said. He glanced at the wall clock. Usually, his grandfather was out helping with chores this time of day.

"Now, I know you're wondering why I'm not out with the fellas," Gramps began. "But the rain has my arthritis squawking. Thought I'd help the boss in the house today." He inclined his head toward Bess.

In response, Bess groaned loudly. "*Oh, please.* I've got cinnamon rolls in the oven. That's why he's here."

"Merely a coincidence. But can you blame me?" Gramps looked at Drew for support. "Your brothers ate them all before I got back from town last time. I'm staking my claim. Nothing wrong with that."

Drew jumped in before the duo could continue. "Bess, maybe you should sit down. I need to discuss something with both of you."

"Oh, dear. Now you have me worried." Frowning, her lips a thin line, Bess wiped her hands on a towel and moved to the kitchen table.

Drew glanced at both of their concerned faces. There was no way to ease into the explanation.

"What is it, son?" Gramps nudged.

"I've been named temporary guardian of Jase and Delia's baby." The words slipped out in a rush. "Well, not just me. Also Delia's best friend, Sadie Ross. You might remember her from the wedding." Relieved to share the remarkable events of the last few hours, he pulled out a chair and sat down. "We've decisions to make about a more permanent situation. Just not today."

"Well, I'll be." Gramps leaned back in his chair, a grin on his face.

Bess gasped, and her eyes widened with delight. "A baby!" The response was a combination of an exclamation and a sigh of pleasure.

Questions fell like rain, and Drew tried to answer them all. Finally, he raised a palm in the air. "They're out in the truck."

"Andrew Scott Morgan. You left a woman and a baby out in the cold?" Gramps sputtered.

"The engine is running, and the heater is on."

"Bring them on in," Bess said. "I don't bite, and Gus here doesn't most of the time."

Drew pointed to his grandfather. "First. Some ground rules."

"You're giving me rules?" Gramps snorted. "I'm eighty

years old. That makes me your elder, not the other way around."

"I know. I know, Gramps. But this is serious. Sadie's a bit skittish. Give her some time to get to know you. And don't talk too much about Jase and Delia. Not today, at least." He paused. "Oh, and as it turns out, Sadie knows less about babies than I do. Try not to mention that either."

Gramps blinked. "Don't suppose I can talk about the weather."

"That's probably safe, so long as you don't bring up twisters," Drew said.

Bess shook her head. "I'll keep him in line. Don't you worry, Drew." The industrial-sized stainless-steel oven beeped, and she stood. "Perfect timing. We'll have coffee and cinnamon rolls."

By the time Drew had picked up a sleeping baby and ushered Sadie into the house, the table had a fresh tablecloth and an enticing spread ready. Bess and Gramps stood waiting with eager smiles on their faces. Both of their eyes lit up at the sight of Mae.

"Sadie, this is my grandfather, Gus Morgan. You may have met him at the…the, um, the wedding. And our family friend Bess Lowder. Bess keeps the household running for us."

"Pleased to meet you, Sadie." Gramps grinned as he offered a handshake.

Sadie took his hand with a shy smile.

"What a treat to have another female. Two females." Bess chuckled as she zeroed in on Mae in Drew's arms. "I've been outnumbered for years. Now I have a fighting chance."

The comment broke the ice, and Sadie's shoulders relaxed. "Do you live here also?" she asked.

"May as well. I'm here most of the time." She smiled.

"But no. I have a place down the road. It's too much house for one person, but I haven't had the time to think about downsizing."

Sadie nodded while Mae babbled in response, her little arms and legs in motion.

"Let's get this dolly out of that jacket," Bess said. "May I hold her?" She shot Drew a pointed look. "Extra cinnamon rolls for you if you say yes."

Drew laughed at the bribe. "Sure." Bess always saved him extra cinnamon rolls as a routine. It was her way of thanking him for helping her when she needed assistance on her property.

"Now, ya'll, take a seat," Bess said. She looked at Sadie. "You're in for a treat. I make the best cinnamon rolls in three counties. You can take that to the bank."

"She's modest too." Gramps snorted.

Drew glanced at Sadie, who seemed entranced by the scene unfolding before her. Was it really going to be this easy? For some reason, he'd figured things wouldn't measure up to her gentrified standards, yet her face reflected the opposite.

"Coffee, Sadie?" Bess asked.

"Yes, please." She ate quietly, all the while observing the interactions between Bess and Gramps, looking mesmerized. True to his word, Drew's grandfather kept the conversation away from potential land mines.

"That was the best cinnamon roll I've ever had." Sadie wiped her mouth with a cloth napkin and addressed her next remark to Bess and Gramps. "Thank you both for welcoming me into your home."

"Our pleasure," Gramps said with a grin.

Sadie smiled. "May I use your ladies' room?"

Bess directed her, and once Sadie was out of earshot,

Gramps leaned forward in his chair. "What are you going to do about this situation?"

"Gramps, it's been three hours since we picked up Mae. All I want to do is get Sadie and Mae settled here in the house. Then we'll figure it out."

"How long will Sadie be with us?" Bess asked.

Drew shook his head. "I'm not sure of that either."

"You've got that cattle association meeting tonight," Gramps said.

"I know. Sam will have to go."

Gramps quirked a brow. "Knowing your brother, he won't be too happy."

"Yeah, well, I wasn't thrilled to have to cover for him last month when he followed that barrel racer up to the Vancouver rodeo. I don't want to hear about it."

Drew picked up his second pastry and took a bite. At least some things didn't change. Bess's cinnamon rolls, slathered with cream cheese icing and oozing butter, could negotiate world peace.

"Sadie is lovely," Bess said.

"Huh?" Mouth full, Drew slowly turned in his chair to face Bess, who rocked Mae against her ample form.

"I said Sadie's lovely. Don't you think?" she asked with a knowing smile.

He shook his head and quickly chewed and swallowed. "Nope. Don't go there."

"All I said…"

"Yes. Sadie is a nice woman. End of story." Drew took a swig of coffee and studied the crumbs scattered across his plate.

"Not your usual type," Gramps observed as he stood. He sauntered over to the counter and poured himself another cup of coffee before sitting down once again.

"My usual type?" Warning bells sounded at the words,

and Drew straightened in his seat. It would be a mistake to let down his guard around his wily grandfather.

"Oh, you know. The kind that needs rescuing."

"What are you talking about?" Drew stared at the family patriarch, annoyance brewing.

"Remember that Taylor woman you took out who kept crying about how her fiancé dumped her? Or that down-on-her-luck widow-lady. What was her name?"

"It doesn't matter. I'm not dating Sadie, and your evaluation's way off the mark."

"Is it?" Gramps raised his bushy brows. "One hundred women in the room, and you'll find the only H & H."

"H & H?" Drew already regretted the query. He usually knew better than to stand in range of his grandfather's punch line.

"Headache and heartache."

Drew's jaw sagged, and he found himself without a reply. Did he dare think further on his grandfather's assessment?

A moment later, Sadie walked into the room and looked around the table. "Did I miss something?"

"Nope. Not a thing," Drew said. He turned to Bess. "Would you mind Mae while Sadie and I get things moved into the house from my truck?"

"Hmm." Bess smiled down at Mae and gently pushed the wisps of fine blond baby hair to the side of her forehead. "Let me think. Wash dishes or snuggle with a cute child who smells like a little bit of heaven. That's a tough choice."

As Sadie and Drew stepped outside, Sadie paused. "I got the distinct impression that I walked into the middle of something back there."

"Nothing but the usual Morgan household hijinks." He pointed to the truck, hoping to change the subject real fast.

"Let's get things inside. According to the schedule in Delia's binder, Mae's going to want to eat again soon. The baby food jars are buried somewhere in there."

Sadie followed him to the vehicle, where he released the tailgate and uncovered the tarp protecting Mae's essential supplies. She shook her head. "I would have never thought that when I left Tulsa, I'd be adding the care and feeding of a six-month-old to my skill set."

"I'm right there with you," Drew said. He grabbed the crib and hauled it to the ground. "You and Mae will be on the first floor," he said. "Near the back of the house. Less foot traffic."

"Does that mean I'm the designated middle-of-the-night caregiver?" she asked. The fret-face had returned.

"Helen said she sleeps through the night." Drew paused. "I thought it would be quieter for her naps and for you as well." He searched her face, realizing he probably should have discussed the situation with her first. Fact was, as ranch manager, he was accustomed to making quick decisions.

"I'm sorry. You're right," Sadie said. "I'm overthinking. That will be perfect, thank you." She nodded. "That reminds me. I called my department head while I was waiting in the truck. We scheduled a video conference for tomorrow at nine."

"I'll tell Gramps and Bess to keep the noise down."

"I appreciate that." She grabbed a lamp and a box of diapers and headed into the house.

Even Drew was surprised when an hour later, the room was set up and ready for Mae.

Sadie sat in a rocker and glanced around. "It resembles her old room."

"Yeah." Drew nodded. "It does. I'll grab the rest of her things tomorrow, but this works for now."

"Whose room was this?" she asked.

"Used to be my mother's sewing room, and your room was the guest room. This part of the house was remodeled to add the guest bathroom."

"How many bedrooms are upstairs?"

"Four. My room. Gramps is in my folks' old room. Sam had his own room. Then my youngest brothers, who are fraternal twins, shared a room."

"Do you mind if I ask what happened to your parents?"

A frisson of dread shot through Drew at the question. After all these years, he still couldn't discuss his parents as though it was simply another chapter in his life. Maybe that was why losing Jase hit him so hard. Why he related to Mae's situation.

"We lost them the year I graduated from college. Car accident."

Sadie released a small gasp. "I'm so sorry."

Drew waved a hand of dismissal. It wasn't a topic he liked to dwell on. Everyone had a story. That was life.

"It was a long time ago," he said. "The Morgans have family spread from one end of Oklahoma to the other end. They all stepped up to help. And Gramps moved in with us." He paused. "The Lord took care of everything, and in the end, it all worked out."

"In the end," Sadie mused. "Do you believe in happy endings, Drew?"

"Sure," he said. "But it's a choice. Not like a gift someone gives you. You have to choose to have a happy ending."

For moments, silence stretched between them. Finally, Drew worked up the courage to address the thought niggling in the back of his mind. "Okay if I ask you a personal question?"

"Sure."

"What's the story with you and Delia? You were in the same foster family?"

"No. We met in a group-home setting."

He pondered the answer. Technically, he and his brothers were orphans. The difference was that he had family coming out of his ears—more family than he knew what to do with most days. "You lived in a group home. Not with a family?"

"That's correct," she said matter-of-factly. "In Tulsa, until we aged out at eighteen."

"When you turned eighteen." He couldn't hide the surprise in his voice as he put it all together. What a birthday present. Happy birthday, and there's the door.

"Uh-huh." She abruptly averted her face, clearly ending the conversation.

"I'm sorry, Sadie," he murmured.

She gave a tight-lipped nod of acknowledgment at the words.

The clop-clop of boots coming down the hallway had both Drew and Sadie turning their heads. Gramps appeared a moment later. He cocked his head toward the kitchen. "Bess said Mae is hungry. Wants to know if it's okay to mix up some mashed sweet potatoes or bananas."

Sadie reached for the baby binder on the bureau and searched the list of foods. "Both are on the approved list."

"Alrighty, I'll tell her." Gramps shot both Drew and Sadie a pointed look. "You two best come along and observe. Next round is yours."

"He's right," Drew said once his grandfather was out the door.

Sadie nodded in agreement, her face somber. "We both should commit this binder to memory."

"Sounds like a crash course in Baby 101 with no prerequisites." Drew chuckled. "Is there going to be a test?"

Sadie stiffened. "I'm serious here. I've already started reading. Did you know that Mae has a ventricular septal defect? I wonder why Delia never mentioned it."

"A heart defect?" His chest tightened. "That sounds serious."

She nodded. "Delia's notes say that it's a hole in the lower chamber of the heart." She flipped a page. "It's expected to resolve as she gets older. Helen said so earlier, but she called it a minor issue…"

"Okay," he said with a nod. "So maybe it's not as serious as it sounds. Wouldn't Helen or our friends have mentioned it if it was?" He ran a hand through his hair. "Then again, what do we know? We aren't her real parents, and we sure aren't doctors."

"Mae has a heart defect, Drew. It sounds serious to me. Maybe even more serious than you and I can handle." She looked overwhelmed.

"Easy." He raised a palm. "We don't have to sort that now. She has us. And with Bess around too, little Mae is in good hands."

"Yes. I've already said a few prayers of thanks for Bess. But she won't be around all the time. She said she has her own place."

"Bess arrives Monday through Friday between nine and ten. At noon, she brings lunch out to the barn for the wranglers. After chores around the house, she takes the ranch truck, heads to town and grabs the mail."

"You don't have mail delivery?"

"This is rural Oklahoma. We have to pick it up at the post office." He continued, "Once Bess gets back to the ranch, she has dinner in the oven or the fridge before she leaves for the day. We're on our own Saturday and Sunday."

"What about your brothers?"

"Most nights, they show up for dinner, but I'm sending

Sam to the Cattleman's Association meeting tonight, and the twins are headed to Oklahoma City for a concert after they finish their chores. They'll all be here on Friday."

"You two coming?" Gramps called.

"On the way," Drew said.

As he moved toward the doorway, Sadie put a hand on his arm. Drew turned. "Are you okay?" he asked.

"Yes." She released a soft breath, the dark eyes intent. "What are we doing, Drew?"

He took a moment to answer, knowing he couldn't and wouldn't sugarcoat the situation. "We're taking it one step at a time, Sadie. I don't know how to do anything else."

One step at a time.

He'd repeated the phrase to himself over and over for the last few hours. Maybe soon, he'd find comfort in the words.

"Leah, can you hear me?" Sadie repeated. Frustration simmered as the picture on her laptop pixilated, and the sound vanished. The connection at the Lazy M Ranch left something to be desired, and she really needed this face-to-face meeting with Leah Telfer, her department head, to explain her current predicament.

A moment later, as quickly as the picture had deteriorated, it was restored.

"Good morning, Sadie." Leah grinned.

"Good morning," Sadie replied. The middle-aged department head was not only her supervisor but her friend as well, and touching base helped reduce Sadie's stress level.

Leah angled her head to have a better look at the room behind Sadie. "So, you're on a ranch, right? Where exactly?"

"Lazy M Ranch in Homestead Pass, Oklahoma. It's a small town in far western Oklahoma. About three hours from Tulsa."

"Hmm. I haven't stepped outside of Tulsa County so far." She smiled and offered a mischievous grin. "Have you seen any cowboys?"

Sadie nearly laughed aloud at the unexpected question, but Leah was a recent transplant from Connecticut and fascinated by all things Western. She'd been sorely disappointed when she hadn't found cowboys in suburban Tulsa.

"A few," Sadie returned.

"Oh? Now I'm intrigued. Tell me what's happening on the ranch," Leah continued.

As if on cue, Mae's crying in the next room filled the air. It was followed by the now-familiar sound of boots on wood and the shuffle of movement down the hall. No doubt, Gramps and Bess were racing to see who could pick up the crying baby first. Bess had arrived early this morning, motivated by her delight with little Mae. Disappointed that the baby was still asleep, she lamented that none of her children had the good sense to give her a grandchild yet.

"Do I hear a baby?" Leah asked.

"Um, yes," Sadie returned weakly.

"Whose baby?"

"Mine. Sort of."

Leah frowned, clearly perplexed. "Excuse me?"

Sadie quickly explained the situation, grateful for a friend with whom she could share her heart.

"Oh, my." Leah's eyes became watery. "I know this must be an emotional time, and there are many decisions to be made. Please know that as your department head and friend, I'm here for you."

Relief swept through her. "Thanks, Leah. I appreciate that."

"So, you're a new parent," Leah said. "How about that."

Sadie blinked. A parent? Since she'd left the attorney's

office, the word *guardian* had been all she'd considered. Being called a parent seemed far more daunting.

"Sadie, you may not be aware that the college prides itself on being a family-friendly employer," Leah said. "They offer up to eight weeks of paid parental leave for the birth or adoption of a child. I have no doubt that your situation will qualify." Leah paused. "Shall we submit the paperwork and find out?"

Eight weeks? Sadie hesitated. What about her classes? Her apartment? She didn't like uncertainty. Her past had been punctuated by uncertainty. No, she preferred to stay in control.

"I'm not sure. Everything has happened so quickly," she finally admitted on an uneven breath. "For now, I'd like to use my vacation days to take some time off. I want to be here for Mae's cardiology appointment. May I get back to you on Monday?"

"Certainly, but the sooner, the better." Leah flipped through the pages of a planner on her desk. "Is there anything else I should know?"

"Not yet."

"All right, but remember, you have a very competent teaching assistant. I know how precise you are, but this is the time to delegate."

Sadie nodded. She could delegate. Sure, she could.

"The family-leave option is on the table. Fill out the paperwork and then I encourage you to take it if you need it."

"Thank you, Leah."

A light tap sounded on the door behind her. "Sadie?" Drew called.

"Excuse me, Leah." Sadie turned in her chair. "Come in."

Drew cracked the door and peeked into the room. His brows shot up. "My apologies for the interruption. I guess I thought your meeting would be over."

"No worries," she said. "We had to move the meeting."

He handed her a plastic shopping bag. "Bess picked up those supplies you needed."

"Wonderful. Thank you."

He nodded and offered a tip of his Stetson as he backed out of the room and closed the door.

"Be still my heart," Leah said. "A cowboy. We don't see those running around on the campus of Tulsa College."

"That was Drew Morgan. He's Mae's other guardian." Sadie's mind jumped to Leah's comment.

Parent.

At least for now, Drew was Mae's other *parent.* Every hour, the reality of the situation became more and more surreal. She, a woman with no experience in the child-care department, hoped to become a permanent guardian. Well, whatever it took, she would do it. Because saving Mae from a childhood in foster care, like she and Delia had experienced, was her mission.

"So, you're staying on a ranch with a cowboy," Leah murmured.

Sadie turned her attention back to the screen.

An impish smile curved Leah's lips as she slipped on oversize black-framed glasses. She clearly found amusement in the situation. "That sounds intriguing."

"Not as much as you'd think. Drew's grandfather and the housekeeper are also here, along with the baby." Sadie sighed. "And the rest of the Morgan family, ranch hands and cows. Lots of cows." She glanced out the guestroom window, where the cows she'd spotted this morning continued to graze beneath a cloudless spring sky.

"I'm going to need pictures, Sadie. Text me a few."

Sadie chuckled. "Sure."

"And we'll touch base again on Monday?"

Sadie nodded, and they ended the call.

Monday. Three days from now to make decisions that would affect the rest of her life. Maybe the extra time she had asked for would be enough to learn how to be a mother, if she started studying right away.

Sadie picked up the framed photo of her and Delia that she'd borrowed from the Franklin house. "I'll do the right thing, sweet friend." She choked back emotion. "You never let me down and I won't let your little girl down. I promise."

Reaching for the baby notebook, Sadie checked Mae's schedule. Lunch hour and her turn for feeding duty. Her first time.

Sadie walked down the hall to the kitchen while pushing away concerns and mentally prepping herself for the task. There was nothing as challenging as teaching a bored senior class the week before graduation. She'd survived that by standing her ground. Feeding a baby ought to be easy peasy in comparison. Or so she kept telling herself.

Sadie stopped short in the kitchen doorway at the sight of Mae in a high chair slapping her pudgy little hands on the tray and chortling while Drew soared a spoonful of mashed peas through the air like an airplane. After a few approaches, the spoon landed in Mae's mouth.

The cowboy no longer wore his Stetson but had donned an orange-and-black OSU ball cap, and he seemed to be thoroughly enjoying the task. And Sadie enjoyed watching him. He was a big guy who ought to be awkward feeding a tiny human. But he wasn't. No, Drew Morgan had a confidence and ease of movement she envied.

"You're feeding her," Sadie finally said. Torn between indignation and relief, she wasn't sure what to do. After all, she only had so much training time, yet she wasn't looking forward to another opportunity to make a fool of herself in front of the cowboy.

Drew glanced at Sadie and shrugged. "Yeah, sorry, but the princess made her demands clear." He spooned another bit of food into the baby's mouth. "Only a few mouthfuls left."

Mae looked at Sadie, and her face contorted into a grimace before she spit up the peas.

"I'm making her gag."

He released a chuckled. "It's not you. It's the peas. You're taking this way too personally."

"Am I?" Sadie raised her brows. "Let's discuss my first and second disastrous diaper changes."

After wiping a blob of green from Mae's chin, he began another plane takeoff. "Last one, munchkin." When he'd finished, he turned to Sadie. "Mae senses that you're nervous."

"Hello? That's because I am nervous."

"The key is to fake it." Drew looked up at her again, his expression compassionate.

Sadie glanced away. She did not do sympathy. Eager to change the subject, she found a reprieve in the pile of books on the counter. "My books have arrived." Hope immediately replaced her anxiety.

"Those are yours? Ha. I should have known." He wiped Mae's mouth and the tray table before he stood. "Where did you get them?"

Sadie frowned at his comment. What was wrong with books? "I called the bookstore last night and talked to the owner, Mrs. Pickett. She said she'd have someone run them by."

"Nice of her." He eyed the stack again. "That's a lot of baby books."

"I thought you and I could take turns reading them."

Surprise flickered in his eyes. "You want me to read a baby book? I haven't even finished Delia's notebook."

"I haven't either. Then again, it's only been twenty-four hours." She ran a loving hand over the bindings. "However, these books will fill the gap in our education."

Drew stood at the sink, frowning, obviously unimpressed with her suggestion. "What's wrong with hands-on education?"

"Why fake it, as you put it, when we have access to expert knowledge?"

"Good thing I'm not the sensitive kind," he said. "Or I might think you just insulted me."

"That's not what I meant. I'm an academic. Books are my lifeblood."

"Yeah, I can see that." He turned on the faucet and rinsed the feeding spoon. "I prefer living life instead of reading about it."

Sadie bristled at the response that hit far too close to home. "Fine."

"I can read the books, Sadie."

"Don't do it on my account." She shrugged. "Oh, and I went online and ordered a dry-erase board to track Mae's schedule."

"Books. A dry-erase board. That sounds like you're sticking around."

"I'm simply organized." Her response was neither an admission nor a commitment to anything.

"Yeah. You are organized. I'll give you that." Drew frowned yet again. "And I'm a little confused. Seems to me we have a simple decision to make. Which one of us will accept primary guardianship of Mae?"

"I'm going to need a little more time to prep before making a decision." She waved a hand toward the books. "Thus, the books and the schedule tracking."

"You talked to your boss. Surely, you discussed Mae."

"I did."

"And?"

Sadie hesitated. Did she really want to admit that Leah offered her the possibility of eight more weeks? Eight weeks in Homestead Pass.

No. Not yet.

Sadie looked at the stack of books once again. They were her lifeline. The only possible way she could learn childcare and make an informed decision about which of them was the best choice for Mae's permanent guardian.

"I've had a week more vacation time approved," she finally said. That was the absolute truth. Leah had agreed to her taking the extra time off.

"A week?" Drew's face brightened, creases forming around his eyes as a grin appeared. "That will take you through Mae's cardiology visit. I appreciate you doing that."

"We're both making sacrifices, right?" She raised her shoulders in acknowledgment, all the while feeling guilty for her lack of full disclosure.

"Yeah."

"By the way, is there any way you can upgrade the internet situation so it's reliable? I'm going to need to meet online with my teaching assistant this week."

"Sure. I'll look into that right away."

Sadie picked up a squeaky toy that Mae had tossed onto the floor. "What about you? Have you come up with any ideas?"

"I've been thinking about schedules as well." He placed the lid on the jar of baby food. "I can shift some of my duties around. That way, one of us is always here with Mae."

"And when our schedules conflict?" Sadie asked.

"I'm sure Bess will help us out. She's itching to."

Sadie looked around. "Where is Bess?"

"It's noon. She took the UTV and brought lunch out

to the barn. Gramps went with her, following the trail of food."

Drew moved over to the counter and examined the books one by one. "What sort of degree do you have?"

"A PhD in Literature. My area of specialty is Shakespearean studies."

"Say what? You're a doctor?" He blinked, and his jaw sagged. "Seriously?"

"I have a doctorate. Yes. Is that a problem?" She found herself on the defense, which often happened when she shared details of her life's work.

"No. But it's sort of like a rancher with an architecture degree. Turns out it's useless on a ranch. What do you do with a PhD in literature specializing in Shakespearean studies?"

Sadie stiffened at the comment. "Teach. I teach."

"Ever think of doing something else?" Drew asked.

She cocked her head at the random query. "Yes."

He raised his palms in question.

A small huff slipped from Sadie's lips at the man's bold persistence. "If you must know. I wanted to go into medicine. However, it turns out that I'm squeamish." She hated admitting such a ridiculous weakness. Who fainted at the sight of blood? She did.

"Shakespeare was your alternative career path?"

Sadie opened her mouth to answer and then closed it again. Where was he going with all the questions?

"I love teaching, and I love literature." She paused and stared at him. "Are you trying to annoy me? Or do these questions have a point?"

"Sadie, we're two near strangers plopped into someone else's life. Don't you think it would be good to get to know each other?"

For a moment, Sadie simply studied the cowboy. His

expression remained serious. She couldn't figure the man out, though she had to admit that she hadn't expected him to be struggling with the same questions that kept her pacing the floor last night.

They were from two different worlds, forced together because of their friends and a baby.

"What do you think?" he asked.

"You're right," she admitted. For better or worse, they were in this together. Sadie shivered at the admission.

Chapter Three

"It's generous of you to stay, Bess." Sadie dried another plate and put it in the cupboard while addressing the house-keeper.

"All the Morgan boys will be here for dinner tonight. I couldn't throw you into that lion's den without a little backup." Bess rinsed a mixing bowl and added it to the growing pile of clean dishes in the drainer before she turned to Sadie. "We girls have to stick together. Right?"

Sadie smiled, warmed by the camaraderie Bess offered. "Absolutely."

It was twenty minutes until dinner, and the scents emanating from the oven had Sadie's stomach growling. "That lasagna you made smells amazing."

"Not me. *We* made it. You can add lasagna Bolognese to your repertoire."

"Just between us, I don't have a repertoire." Sadie gave a short, embarrassed laugh. "Unless you count avocado toast. I can make four varieties of that."

"Avocado toast. Never heard of it." Bess turned from the sink to look at Sadie, a puzzled expression on her face. "You're telling me no one ever taught you how to cook?"

"Correct. Though I am a whiz with the microwave."

Sadie was loath to mention her upbringing or the fact that the group home utilized a meal planning service.

"The microwave?" A horrified expression crossed Bess's face. "Babies and children need the nutrition that comes from real food, not those frozen, dehydrated packages." She clucked her tongue. "Have you ever tried to cook from scratch?"

Sadie shrugged. "For one person? I never saw the point in cooking, period."

The other woman's eyes widened.

"It's not a matter of ability. I feel certain I could cook if it were necessary. It's never been necessary."

Bess gave a slow, sad shake of her head. "I can see I have my work cut out for me."

Sadie smiled. "Are you suggesting teaching me how to cook?"

"Honey, I'm not suggesting. I'm *telling* you. If you live on a ranch, cooking is a necessity. You've mastered lasagna. Next, we'll prepare baby food."

"We brought baby food from Delia's house."

Indignation flashed in Bess's eyes. "Like I said. Next, we'll prepare baby food."

"Bess, I only have a short time at the ranch. I'm due back in the classroom soon after Mae's doctor appointment."

"A week with me." She grinned. "You'll be an expert in no time."

Sadie perked up at the words and glanced at Mae, who sat quietly in her high chair playing with a toy. "Did you hear that, Mae? An expert." The baby's head bobbed, and she shoved the tail of the soft rubber cow into her mouth as though she understood.

Mastering homemade baby food would undoubtedly help Sadie's credibility as a candidate for permanent guardianship.

"And I'll tell you a secret," Bess said. "I'm taking Italian cooking classes one night a week at the community center in downtown Homestead Pass."

"Oh?"

"If you're going to be around for a week, you should come with me on Thursday."

"I don't know." She didn't like to tackle anything until she'd completed her due diligence first—studying a topic to lay the groundwork for success.

"You can observe if you like," Bess added.

"That I can do." Sadie felt buoyed by the offer. It did sound like fun now that the risk of failure had been withdrawn.

"Wonderful."

Anxiety kicked in when Sadie's gaze landed on the round farmhouse clock. "Um, so who will be here for dinner tonight?"

"Gus and Drew, as usual. And the boys, Sam, Trevor and Lucas."

Sadie swallowed. She ate her meals alone, hiding in her office at the college during the week. This would be a full house. Yet, she'd known this was coming, so why was she rattled? Perhaps because the thought of four men like Drew Morgan was terrifying.

"You all right?" Bess asked. "You're a bit pale."

"All good." Sadie smiled weakly. "So, Sam is the second eldest."

"That's right. He handles the ranch finances. That boy is a math whiz. If there's a number involved, so is Sam."

"Trevor and Lucas are twins." Sadie repeated what Drew told had her when she'd first arrived.

"Fraternal. Those two are as different as can be." Bess released a musing chuckle.

"How so?"

"Lucas is an extrovert. Spends half the year bustin' broncs. That boy has been a handful from day one. Now, Trevor, well, he's had a few challenges come his way. He's the opposite of Luc in temperament." Bess frowned as though debating whether to share more. "And then Gus, of course."

"Gus is the owner of Lazy M Ranch?"

"Oh, no." Bess shook her head. "It was his son who started the Lazy M. Drew manages the ranch, and he and his brothers equally own the operation. Gus is what you'd call a figurehead."

"Figurehead?"

"Uh-huh. Drew sends him to do all the handshaking he doesn't want to do. Civic events and all. Gus loves schmoozing. That's his element, so to speak."

"Sure. Okay. I can see that. Gus seems very much a people person."

Bess nodded.

"What about Drew?" The question was out of her mouth before Sadie could stop herself.

"The man is a nut that's near impossible to crack." The housekeeper paused and leaned close. "I have my thoughts, mind you, they're only thoughts. Drew loves this ranch, but I don't believe he intended to spend the rest of his life here. He had his suitcase packed and a diploma in his hand, all set to start an internship when his folks died."

"How long has it been since they passed?"

"Nineteen years next month. Sam had just graduated from high school, and the twins were about thirteen."

"So, he stayed." Sadie sighed at Bess's words, empathizing with Drew's losses.

"Yes. That's our Drew. Always does the right thing."

Sadie pondered the words for a moment. She didn't

know Drew well enough to draw any conclusions from Bess's comment. Yet, she couldn't help but wonder.

Drying the last plate, Sadie looked around the kitchen. "All done. What else can I do to help with dinner?"

"Not a thing. We're all set." Bess grabbed an overly ripe banana from the counter, broke off half and mashed it in a small bowl. Then she placed a lump of the mushed-up mixture on Mae's high-chair tray. "This girl loves nanners."

As if agreeing, Mae slapped her palm on the little pile and then touched her mouth eagerly.

"Isn't that going to make a mess?" Sadie asked.

"Absolutely. But that's how babies learn. Right now, we want Mae to get it into her mouth. She'll get the hang of how the thumb and forefinger work in a couple of months, and then she'll pick up solid food."

As Bess spoke, Mae palmed another bit of banana into her mouth and beamed.

The housekeeper laughed. "When all is said and done, we'll just put her in the sink and hose her down."

Sadie looked from Mae to the floor, working to hide her shock. *Hose her down?*

Bess reached over and patted Sadie's arm. "Really, honey. It's all right."

"And here I've been working to keep her meals tidy."

"Nope. Six-month-old babies are learning to enjoy the feel of food. In their mouth and their hands." She shrugged. "Put a trash liner on the floor if it makes you feel better. Though I'm here to tell you, that floor has to be cleaned after dinner anyhow. The boys are nearly as messy as Mae is."

"But you aren't here to clean up after dinner normally."

"That's right. And those boys know what I expect. There won't be cinnamon rolls when I'm perturbed. So, the floor is clean, and the sink is empty when I arrive each morning."

Sadie stared at the tidy dinner table. Plates had been set out, along with silverware and cloth napkins. When the oven buzzed, Bess turned off the timer. After donning gloves, she removed the first casserole and placed it on a cast-iron trivet in the center of the table. Then she took out a second one and left it on the stove.

Boots pounding down the hallway and rowdy male laughter signaled the Morgan brothers were on the way.

"You best stand back," Bess said. "They'll need access to the powder room to wash up. I find that it's safest to give them space and stand downwind. They've been working all day." She scrunched up her nose and shuddered.

"Yes, ma'am," Sadie said.

Drew was the first to enter. He removed his cowboy hat and offered a nod. Bess was right. A fine layer of red dust covered his arms and boots. As his brothers entered the country kitchen, jostling each other and bantering, Drew raised a hand to quell the noise. "Pipe down, would you?"

Sadie pressed her lips together at his commanding words. The silence was immediate. Drew might be a laid-back guy, but he was definitely the leader of this pack.

"I'd like to introduce you to our guests," he continued. "The young lady in the high chair is Miss Mae Franklin. And this is Dr. Sadie Ross."

Sadie offered an embarrassed smile when the brothers removed their dusty hats and offered a solemn greeting one by one.

Drew turned to her. "Sadie, meet the rest of the Morgan family. You know Gramps. These goofs are Sam, Trevor and Lucas."

Sadie had never seen so much testosterone in one room

at the same time. College boys had nothing on these cowboys. The big, sturdy men moved past her to wash up.

Once the kitchen emptied, Bess instructed Sadie to pull
a big bowl of tossed salad and bottled dressings from the
refrigerator. The housekeeper busied herself slicing fresh,
crusty Italian bread.

Minutes later, a *tap tap* echoed from the hallway floor.
Sadie froze when a young dog peered into the kitchen. The
animal looked like a border collie, with a pointed snout and
long red fur with white patches. His pink tongue moved
from side to side as he made a cavalier stroll through the
kitchen, finally stopping in front of Sadie.

From the high chair, Mae remained very still, her corn-
flower-blue eyes big and focused solely on the dog.

"Those boys must have left the front door open," Bess
said with a cluck of her tongue.

"Will he bite?" Sadie asked.

"Cooper?" Bess shook her head. "Nah. The dog doesn't
have a mean bone in him."

The closer the animal got to Sadie, the more she inched
toward Bess, her throat dry and her pulse pounding. She
didn't do well with dogs.

"It's okay," the housekeeper cooed. "You can rub his
forehead. Cooper loves that."

"Oh, I don't know." Touching a dog did not seem like a
good idea. His forehead was much too close to his mouth.

"Go ahead. He's as sweet as can be."

Sadie reached out with slow hesitation to rub Cooper's
head. The thick fur was velvety soft beneath her fingers.
When he leaned into the gesture, she quickly withdrew,
alarmed.

Drew reentered the kitchen and pushed back a lock
of damp hair as he rolled up the sleeves of a clean shirt.
"Lookie there. Cooper likes you. He wants more."

"Are you sure he likes me?" Sadie asked. She felt sure the dog was setting her up before he chomped on her fingers.

Cooper whined.

"Drew's right," Bess said. "He likes you. You're in trouble now."

"Ever have a dog, Sadie?" Drew asked.

"I have not," she said.

Gus stepped into the room. "Cooper, what are you doing in here again?"

"He'd rather be with people than animals," Bess said. "I think you should let him stay here at the house. We could use a porch dog."

"Porch dogs are for retirees. Cooper hasn't earned the right," Gramps said from behind Drew. "If you're gonna bring home strays, you gotta teach 'em the rules." He pointed at Cooper and shook his head. "That pup has a mind of his own. I tell him one thing, and he does whatever he pleases."

"Aw, Cooper just needs a little more training," Drew said. He led the animal out of the kitchen.

Gus released a breath loudly. "Some things never change. That boy has been bringing home strays since he was a kid. He's got a heart a mile wide."

Sadie took in the interaction with interest, tucking the information away as she washed her hands for dinner.

As the brothers filed back into the room, Bess opened the refrigerator once more, pulled out a large pitcher of iced tea and handed it to Gus. "Let's sit down, folks," she said. "Supper is waiting."

When Drew returned, he stared at Lucas, who'd slipped into the chair next to Mae, near the end of the table and across from Sadie. "You're in my seat," he told his little brother.

"I don't see your name on it." Lucas stood and examined the chair before he sat down again. "Nope. Nothing here."

"Seriously? How old are you?"

"Younger than you, *Andrew*. And I want to sit next to the baby."

"Get your own baby," Drew shot back. "This one is mine."

Both Trevor and Sam snickered at the exchange.

Sadie blinked and reached for her water glass as the comments soared past like rubber darts.

"Move, pal," Drew continued, his jaw set and his gaze intimidating.

Lucas stood and straightened to his full height, putting him nose-to-nose with Drew. "Fine. But when I get myself a baby, I'll remember this."

Sadie laughed at the rebuttal, nearly choking on her water.

"You okay, honey?" Bess asked from the seat next to Sadie.

Nodding vigorously, Sadie cautiously eyed the brothers, hoping to remain out of the conversation.

Drew met Sadie's gaze and offered a wink that said, "Watch this."

She did, with rapt attention.

He leaned forward and glanced at his brothers, focusing on Sam, who sat on the other side of Gus. "Hey, Sam, that barrel-racer friend of yours called the house phone."

"What?" Sam's head jerked up. Startled, he nearly dropped his glass of tea. "What did you say?"

"Not a thing, though I gave her your cell number." Drew frowned and cocked his head. "How come you haven't already given it to her?"

"Sam doesn't want her to find out he's no longer riding a bronc but a desk in an office," Luc said. "Right, Sam?"

Sam's gaze spanned the table, where all eyes were on him. He nodded toward the steaming casserole in the middle of the table. "Lasagna looks delicious, doesn't it?"

Drew laughed at the distraction ploy. "Let's pray," he said.

Sadie took Bess's hand and Mae's tiny fist and bowed her head as Drew led them in prayer. When he'd finished, platters started around the table.

"What's for dessert, Bess?" Trevor asked.

"Dessert?" She blinked at the question. "You haven't even put lasagna on your plate yet."

"Does that mean there's no dessert?"

"I learned how to make ricotta cookies in class this week."

Trevor cringed. "Cheese cookies?"

"Don't listen to him. Anything you make is delicious." Lucas leaned over to kiss Bess's cheek. "And remember, I'm going to marry you when I grow up."

At that, the entire table broke into laughter. Sadie hid a laugh as Bess slapped at his hand and shushed the cowboy away. "Oh, go on with you."

"What is it you do back home, Dr. Ross?" Sam asked.

"Sadie. Just Sadie," she said with a smile. "I teach literature at Tulsa College."

"TC. Really? I do a little teaching at OSU when they need me," Sam said.

"Oh?" Sadie's interest was piqued at his response. "What curriculum?"

"Business courses." He handed the salad bowl to Drew as he spoke.

"That's right. Drew said you manage the books at the ranch." She smiled and assessed his rugged features. The man was a cowboy first, an accountant second. "You look nothing like the traditional number cruncher."

"Why, that's the nicest thing anyone's said to me all day." He elbowed Drew. "I like your guest."

Drew raised his brows and once again met Sadie's gaze across the table. "Yeah? Just remember, she's *my* guest."

Sadie's face warmed at the words. She knew the banter was male posturing, yet as the conversation continued and plates emptied, she couldn't help but feel a little like Alice down the rabbit hole. What was this new world she'd been dropped into?

She had a week to figure it out.

"Your technique has improved." Drew leaned against the wall in Mae's room, observing Sadie change the baby's diaper. When she blew strands of hair out of her face and then bit her lip in concentration, he tried not to smile at the scene.

"I hear an *and* in there," Sadie said.

"*And*…the judges agree. This performance was an eight."

"Only an eight? I don't think so."

Inching closer, Drew narrowed his eyes as though inspecting. He couldn't help but give Sadie a hard time. "Hmm."

"I studied. And for the record, this is at least a nine."

"How do you study for putting on disposable diapers?"

"Last night, after your brothers left, I spent a few hours watching online videos." Sadie closed the tabs on the diaper with a flourish. "I did everything exactly as the instructors recommended. Look at those tabs. Perfectly aligned. Please note the absence of gaps or bunching around the legs."

"I'll revise my score to an eight-point-two due to your hard work."

"What?" Outrage laced her voice. "This is at least a nine."

"I'd bump up the score, but you made all sorts of faces the entire time." Drew chuckled at the fire in her dark eyes. "Presentation counts too."

Sadie released a frustrated breath in response. "I made faces because it was an unpleasant diaper."

"Unpleasant diapers happen." He continued to watch her, noting that while she'd become proficient, her confidence hadn't improved.

"You're making me nervous," she said. "Are you still critiquing me?"

"Not at all… By the way, what did you think of my brothers?"

Her face relaxed into a musing smile. "They're charming."

"Fair assessment." Drew chuckled. "They got the Morgan charm from my grandfather."

Sadie put a hand on Mae's forehead and looked up at him with concern. "Drew, she's warm."

Peering closer, he worked to stay calm to keep Sadie calm.

She was correct. Mae's face did seem flushed. Her eyes were a bit glassy as well. He gently stroked the baby's arm. "You're right. And now that I think about it, a couple of the wranglers called in with a bug last week." He glanced around. "Isn't there a thermometer in her bag?"

"Yes." Sadie grabbed the diaper bag and searched inside. "Here." She thrust the digital thermometer kit at him.

"Whoa!" Drew kept his hand on Mae but managed to dodge Sadie's offering. "Why do I have to be the one to check her temperature?"

"Because I'm the one reading the baby books. Besides, the method of application recommended by the experts for that thermometer is not something I am familiar with. Nor do I want to become familiar." She paused. "Ever."

"Don't look at me," he said.

She gave an adamant shake of her head. "You have cows and chickens and horses. You're far better qualified than I am."

Unable to deny the claim, he released Mae and accepted the kit. Yeah, after twenty years as a ranch foreman, he'd handled far more challenging things. However, that didn't mean he wouldn't finesse the situation to his advantage. "Okay, I'll do it." He met her gaze. "If you take my next diaper change."

"What? That's low, Morgan," Sadie sputtered. She put a hand to Mae's head. "Fine. Just hurry. She seems warmer than she did a few minutes ago."

Sadie grabbed one of the baby care books, now stacked on the bureau, and began to flip through the pages while he proceeded with his task.

Drew glanced at her and made a vow to address the division of duties. The arrival of the dry-erase board tomorrow would be a good time for a chat. Parenting, however temporary, ought to be a fifty-fifty proposition. That was how his folks had always handled the job.

"One hundred and one degrees," he announced minutes later. That wasn't good at all. "What's the book say about that?"

She looked up from the pages, her dark eyes round. "According to the physician who runs the pediatric department of one of the biggest hospitals in the country, that's considered a true fever."

"I've never heard of a true fever, but I suggest we get her in to see the pediatrician ASAP."

"Is the Homestead Pass Clinic open on a Saturday?"

"Sure is," he returned.

"I'm going to order a forehead thermometer while you call."

Less than thirty minutes later, all three of them were escorted to a sick-baby examination room at the town clinic. A nursing assistant had taken Mae's vital signs and promised the doctor would be in soon.

The only sound in the stark room was the tick of the industrial clock on the wall. The ticks seemed to grow louder and louder and had him and Sadie exchanging worried glances. Sadie had her fret-face on, and he figured he probably did too.

When Mae began to fuss in the car-seat carrier, they both reached for her simultaneously. Drew's hands tangled with Sadie's.

"Oh, sorry," she said, stepping back.

"Nothing to be sorry about." He eased Mae from the carrier and began to walk around the office, gently jostling the baby in his arms, grateful to have something to do.

While he and Mae strolled, Sadie sat in a hard plastic chair and studied Delia's baby binder. "I'm worried, Drew. Mae's sick and she has a cardiac issue."

He considered her words and worked not to feed into her anxiety. "We're in the right place. They'll take good care of her here. Try not to overreact."

Sadie shook her head. "Okay. Okay. You're right. I'm sure the doctors can handle this, and Tulsa is an excellent resource for specialists."

Was this another plug for taking Mae from Homestead Pass to Tulsa? He looked at her.

"I had a few medical issues as a child," she continued. "It was Delia who stood by me when I had health problems."

"You knew Delia when you were a little kid?"

"Yes. The foster family we lived with decided they'd

keep Delia and return me back to stock. I was too much trouble."

"You were returned?" Drew frowned, stunned at her response. "That's messed up. Who would do that?"

"It's not uncommon." She shrugged as though downplaying her answer. "I had some respiratory problems and multiple allergies. No one wants to deal with that."

Drew searched Sadie's face, but there was no emotion evident. It was as if she was telling someone else's story.

"What happened?" he asked.

"Delia kept running away to find me until they promised to keep us together. We ended up in a managed group home."

He assessed the woman in front of him. She seemed so put together on the outside, but he was beginning to realize that Sadie Ross carried an overflowing trough of pain beneath the surface.

The exam room door opened, and a pleasant-looking woman in a crisp white knee-length lab coat entered the room. "Mr. Morgan. Dr. Ross." She stretched out a hand to each of them in turn and smiled at Mae. "Hello, I'm Dr. Lakhno. I understand you're the guardians."

"Yes, ma'am," Drew said.

"I'm so sorry for your loss. Delia and Jason were such engaged parents. Always eagerly asking questions. I know you feel their loss."

He could only nod.

"So, Mae has a temperature. Would you put her on the exam table, and I'll check things out?" The doctor paused. "And relax, you two. We're a team, and together, we're going to get through whatever comes our way."

Drew had never heard sweeter words. They reminded him who was in charge. Certainly not him. No, the Lord had this.

After a complete exam, Dr. Lakhno looked up and smiled. "Mae is a sweetheart. Even when she feels puny, this little girl gives me a smile."

"What's the verdict, doctor?" Drew asked.

"She has a virus. I'm sure it will pass without problems. We'll draw her blood to ensure we don't miss anything."

"Okay," Drew murmured, working hard not to snatch the situation back from the altar of God he'd placed it on only minutes before.

"Are you aware that a pediatric cardiac specialist follows Mae? Dr. Bedford?"

"Yes," Sadie said. "Mae's grandmother sent us the details of her upcoming appointment."

Dr. Lakhno nodded. "Have you noticed any changes in Mae's breathing or color?"

"We don't have a baseline for noticing changes," Drew said. "She's been living with her grandmother, who seemed to think everything was fine."

"Good. Very good." The physician nodded. "Mae's murmur seems the same, though her weight is down, which is concerning." She typed into a laptop on the counter. "Keep that appointment. Dr. Bedford books months out." She turned to them. "In fact, why don't you give them a call and ask them to reach out if they have any cancellations between now and then."

"Yes, ma'am." Drew nodded. "What's the worst-case scenario here, Doc? I mean, as far as Mae's heart?"

"I'm not the cardiologist, but it's not unlikely that Dr. Bedford will decide to repair the defect in light of Mae's weight loss."

"Surgery?" Sadie gasped. "On a baby?"

"Yes." The doctor's tone was calm as she added, "But let's not get ahead of ourselves."

"Why didn't Mae's parents mention the condition to us?" Sadie asked.

"Perhaps because they weren't alarmed. The statistics show that one out of every two hundred and forty babies born in this country have this defect. So, it's not an unusual condition, often self-resolving. A watch-and-see situation."

"Any special instructions between now and when Mae sees the cardiologist?" Drew asked.

"This virus should pass in twenty-four to forty-eight hours." Dr. Lakhno recited care instructions and symptoms to watch for. "If you observe anything I mentioned, go straight to the emergency room."

"Yes, ma'am," he said.

"Did you get all that?" Sadie asked him once the physician left the room.

"No. My head was spinning from the idea of heart surgery. We'll ask for a copy of instructions on the way out."

Minutes after Dr. Lakhno left, a phlebotomist came in. Sadie took one look at the tray that carried supplies for a blood draw and paled. "I need to step out of the room."

"You okay?" Drew asked.

"I will be."

By the time she returned, the phlebotomist had completed the blood draw and departed. "Everything go okay?" she asked.

"Mae wasn't thrilled, but it's done." Drew frowned as the pressure of deciding the future for his friend's baby smacked him square in the face. "Cardiology appointment in what? A week and a half? We don't even know what our situation will be after that. You may be gone." He released a breath and shook his head. "And what if she needs surgery? What then?"

Sadie fiddled with the buttons on her sweater. "I do have an option."

"An option. What do you mean?" He cocked his head.

"The college has a parental leave plan. They offer up to eight weeks."

Drew stared at her, baffled at her admission. "When were you going to mention that?"

"When it became important."

Seriously? He couldn't believe his ears. "Because becoming a guardian to a six-month-old wasn't important enough?"

"That's not what I mean. You're misinterpreting my words. I thought this process was going to be simple." She waved a hand as she explained. "And I'd hoped I wouldn't need to stay in Homestead Pass any longer than a week or so."

"I'm going to try not to take offense to the Homestead Pass part of your little speech. But you ought to know I was serious about wanting to be Mae's guardian. It's my opinion that she belongs here. Period."

Sadie's eyes widened though she said nothing in apparent stunned silence. Even Mae stopped fussing for a moment.

Now he'd gone and done it. His brain let the words slip past his mouth, and already Drew regretted his outburst and tone.

Drew ran a hand over his face, feeling the shame of his misstep. "Look, I apologize. There's no excuse for my being sharp with you. Truth be told, I'm overwhelmed."

Sadie nodded, and her shoulders sagged as though she carried a heavy weight. "We both need some time to process today and the future. Let's just go home."

Home. Twenty-four hours ago, life was simple. Now he and a woman he barely knew both called the Lazy M Ranch home. Drew carefully tucked Mae in the carrier and reached for his truck keys. It was definitely time for prayer, because he didn't have a clue what was going on, except that things were out of control.

Chapter Four

Sadie leaned against the back porch rail and looked out at the pasture, willing away the tension that held her shoulders rigid. It had rained again last night, and the moisture in the air brought out the sweet floral scent of blooming lilacs. In the distance, rows of apple trees wore pale pink blossoms like halos. To her left, a huge redbud flanked the porch, its rosy flowers raining to the ground with each passing breeze.

There was no denying how lovely the Lazy M Ranch was in spring. An endless and diverse palette. Her line of sight took in the pastures, stretching to the horizon. The grassland had begun to transform from the browns of winter to the greens of the incoming season.

All of this was so different from her life in Tulsa. Neither good nor bad in comparison. Simply different. It emphasized how small her world had become. Each day, she moved from the college to her apartment, her routine rarely altering.

After all, change had never been her friend.

Sadie picked up the baby monitor from the ground and checked to ensure the volume was on high. Not a sound from the nursery except the quiet ticking of a wall clock.

Once they had returned from the pediatrician's, she'd given Mae a cool bath under Bess's watchful eye and held Mae while Drew administered the fever-reducing liquid medication. The infant had fallen asleep quickly, though Sadie remained in the rocking chair watching until Mae's breathing slowed in slumber.

Welcome to parenting, a small voice in her head whispered. Could she have predicted a week ago that she'd bathe a baby? She nearly laughed aloud at the thought.

"You okay, Miss Sadie?"

Startled, she turned to find Gus at her side. Drew's grandfather offered a comforting smile. "Oh, Gus. I didn't even hear the door open."

"Yeah, I could tell you were deep in thinking mode."

"I guess I was. There are so many decisions to be made," she admitted.

"It's going to be all right, you know."

Sadie released a breath and met his blue eyes. Eyes so like Drew's.

"Will it?" she finally asked.

"Yes, ma'am. Babies are a lot tougher than they look. And, well, the Lord has his hand on the situation."

Sadie nodded absently. She'd have to trust Gus on the baby part. And when it came to the Lord, she knew in her head that the Morgan patriarch was right, even if her heart remained hesitant.

"Are you a believer, Miss Sadie?"

"I am." Faith was what she'd clung to growing up. From the first time she'd picked up a Bible in summer camp, she and Delia had listened to the sermons with growing hunger, especially when she realized that God wouldn't reject her.

"When Miss Mae feels better, you'll visit our little church."

Not a question, but a statement. Sadie smiled at the words. "I'd like that."

"Pastor McGuinness is straight from the old country."

She frowned. "Old country?"

"An Irishman. Like the Morgans."

"*Morgan* is Irish?" The information fascinated Sadie, as she knew precious little about her own heritage. She'd been named by the fireman who found her on the doorstep of Fire Station Five. The oldest fire station in Tulsa. That was the beginning and the end of her historical lineage.

Gus smiled at her question, pride on his weathered face. "*Morgan* means 'sea' and 'circle.' That's the circle of life."

"Now you got him started."

Sadie whirled around at Drew's groaning response. He pushed open the screen door and stepped out to the porch, his boots thunking with each step.

"Did he show you our family crest? Coat of arms?"

"I was just getting to that, wise guy," Gus returned.

"Pace yourself, Gramps. She's going to be here for a bit."

"Is that right?" Speculation laced Gus's drawled words as he turned to Sadie for confirmation.

She nodded, and his face lit up.

"Could you translate 'a bit'?" the older cowboy asked with a smile.

"*A bit* means I'm not sure how long," Sadie admitted.

"Either way, it's good news. Right, Drew?" Gus eyed his grandson and raised his brows suggestively.

"Yes, sir," Drew agreed with a halting expression. A message of sorts passed between the men before Drew cocked his head toward the house.

It seemed the Morgans often communicated without saying a word. Sadie both envied and found herself curious about the nonverbal family language.

"But that's not why I came out here," Drew added. "Bess sent me to let you both know there are sandwiches on the counter."

"That so? What kind?" Gus asked.

"Gramps…" Drew frowned. "Have you ever met a sandwich you don't like?"

"Can't say that I have." The elder Morgan grinned, did an about-face and pulled open the screen door.

"Ready for lunch?" Drew asked Sadie.

"Sure, but things have been so busy today that it's just registering that Bess is here on a Saturday." She paused. "Not that I'm complaining. Quite the opposite."

"I gave her a call from the doctor's office while you were out of the room. I figured we could use the help."

"Thank you."

"No need to thank me. I did it for both of us." Drew held the door open, and as she passed him, the scent of soap and leather teased her senses. She quickened her pace.

"Can you slow down a minute?" Drew called.

She stopped walking and turned.

The tall cowboy stared at his scuffed boots, then raised his head, a determined expression on his face. "I, um… I want to apologize for my tone at the pediatrician's office."

"You already apologized." Sadie met his gaze, noting the concern in his eyes. "You were stressed. I get that."

"There's no excuse for poor behavior," he said. "It won't happen again."

Sadie nodded, unsure what else to say. In the heat of the moment, yes, her feelings had been hurt, but she'd learned long ago to tuck away useless emotional responses. Emotions only added to the pain of circumstances she had no control over.

"Will you be taking the family leave?" he asked.

"I emailed my supervisor, Leah, and told her I would submit the paperwork on Monday."

"Eight weeks in Homestead Pass?" Drew offered a thoughtful nod as though considering all aspects of such a decision.

A wave of panic slammed into Sadie at his response. "If it's approved. And remember, it's a backup plan. That's all." Surely the situation wouldn't warrant that she actually stay here for eight weeks. "I'm sure that soon both of our lives will return to normal."

Drew raised a brow. "Normal? Somehow, I don't think normal is something either of us will see again. Especially since we're no closer to a decision about Mae's guardianship."

"After the cardiac appointment, things will fall into place." Fall into place, meaning she'd be back in Tulsa. Sadie crossed her arms over her chest, feigning the confidence that eluded her at the moment.

"Good to be optimistic," he said.

"Aren't you?"

"Usually, yeah. But I'm still processing." He paused and looked at her, his blue eyes searching. "You know, no one would think any less of you if you decided to allow me to assume primary guardianship. You could visit Mae on the weekends. Wouldn't be much different than before."

"What?" Sadie shook her head. "I don't get you. One minute you're upset that I'm scheduled to leave, and the next, you're encouraging me to go."

"I wasn't at my best at the doctor's office. Truth is, I'm accustomed to being in charge and in control. This is new territory for me."

"Okay. I understand that." Yes, Sadie could well relate to his admission. Though she wasn't simply accustomed to being in control—her mental health depended on being in control. Sadie cleared her throat. "And I can certainly see why you might come to the hasty conclusion that you're more qualified than I am, and that the ranch is a more desirable location to raise a child. However, I want a chance."

"A chance." He scrubbed a hand over his face. "Maybe you can explain what you mean by that."

"I'm trying to say that this is not a competition. I want the same thing you do, Drew. The very best for Delia's baby. Perhaps that's you. Or maybe it's me. I've said it before, and I'll say it again. Whatever we decide, I can promise that ultimately, I'll do what's right for Mae."

Do what's right for Mae.

A groan escaped Sadie's lips the next morning as she raced down the hallway toward the kitchen, her flip-flops slapping against the wooden floor. At the entrance to the kitchen, she screeched to a halt, grabbing the doorframe. Humiliation washed over her at the sight of Drew feeding Mae. Again.

Didn't she feel like a hypocrite? And a failure.

She was supposed to feed Mae this a.m. How had she slept through the alarm? This was so unlike her. Punctuality was her credo, and she demanded as much from her students.

"I'm so sorry. I overslept."

Both Mae and Drew looked up at her.

"No. You slept." Drew smiled and offered Mae another spoonful. "And I'm guessing you did more fretting than sleeping."

"I, ah…" She couldn't deny that it had been a restless night. Yet it was disconcerting that he'd picked up on that. "Want me to take over?" She cocked her head toward Mae.

"Almost done." Drew peered at Sadie's feet. "Interesting footwear you have there."

Sadie glanced at the hot pink flip-flops with faux jewels, and heat rushed to her face. She looked around the kitchen, eager to change the subject and unwilling to admit to a secret penchant for pretty shoes. "It's certainly quiet around here."

"Everyone went to church."

"Oh, yes. Of course. I guess my days are all mixed up."

"Last mouthful, baby girl," Drew crooned. Mae giggled and babbled half words before she opened her mouth agreeably.

If this were a competition, she'd be in trouble. Drew's social game was much better than hers. Sadie frowned. Maybe one of the baby books addressed developing rapport with your child.

"Good job," Drew said.

"How's her temperature?" Sadie placed a gentle hand on Mae's forehead. The baby's blue eyes rounded with surprise, and Sadie smiled as she met Drew's gaze. "It's gone."

He leaned back in the chair and grinned. "Look at you, taking Mae's temperature with your hand like an old pro."

She frowned. Was he teasing her?

"Hey, that was a compliment," he said.

"Uh-huh," she murmured. Picking up the jar of carrots, she examined the container. "Does Bess know she's eating this?"

"What do you mean?"

"Processed baby food." She waved a hand in the direction of the refrigerator. "Bess is pretty adamant about fresh stuff. There's some prepared in the fridge."

"I'll leave that for you." He glanced at his watch. "I've got to get to my chores."

"Chores on a Sunday?" Sadie glanced out the big kitchen window, where the pale blue sky reached down to kiss the treetops.

"Chores are seven days a week on a ranch."

"Why?" She paused at the startled expression on his face. "I mean, it seems that you could organize things so that wouldn't be necessary."

Drew's eyes nearly bugged out, and his jaw sagged. "And it seems you don't know anything about ranch life."

"You're right. My apologies." Sadie quickly retreated from the topic. "Anyhow, I'm sure we can compromise on the food for now."

"Compromise is a good thing."

"Agreed." She bit her lip while considering the next item on her mental to-do list. "Um… There's one more thing."

"Now what?" he asked.

"You said you have chores, but could you spare a few minutes to work on the schedule?"

"No. But I'm guessing I don't have a choice, do I?"

She stiffened. "Of course you have a choice."

"I wanted to discuss this anyway. Let's go into my office," he grumbled. "I'll grab the baby play yard, and the dry-erase board if you handle Mae."

"Deal."

Sadie removed the bib from Mae and wiped the baby's mouth and hands thoroughly. Then she cleaned the feeding tray. As she stepped back, her foot slid.

"Whoa!" Sadie reached for the table ledge to steady herself. A glance at the floor revealed that she'd stepped in a generous dollop of carrot. Standing on one foot, she removed the offending sandal, hobbled to the sink and rinsed the flip-flop before wiping up the mess. Okay, Drew Morgan might be the charming guardian, but she was the guardian who didn't drop food on the floor.

Sadie chuckled softly. There was a bit of self-satisfaction in that knowledge.

"You coming?" Drew called.

"Yes. Yes. Be right there."

She shook the moisture from the sandal, dropped it to the floor and slid her foot in. After plucking Mae from the high chair, Sadie headed down the hall in the direction of Drew's voice. Last Friday, while her mind had grappled with the attorney visit, she'd been given a quick tour of the Morgan house. Now she realized she had no idea where Drew's office was.

"Where are you?" she called.

"End of the hall. Last door on your right."

Sadie entered a room dominated by a massive oak desk and a mesh play yard filled with assorted toys. She placed Mae on the blanket in the play yard and turned around.

"Have a seat," Drew said from behind the desk.

She did and noted the dry-erase board propped on another chair. The board had been divided into days of the week, so Sadie picked up a marker from the chair and quickly added the week's dates.

"I'd like to see an equitable division of labor." The words tumbled out before she lost her courage. "And I recognize that you've been doing more than I have. I'll step up my game."

"Don't be so hard on yourself. You'll have plenty of opportunities because I have a ranch to run. Tomorrow I'll be back on schedule."

"What's your schedule look like?"

"Every single day is different. Usually, I'm out the door doing chores between four and five a.m., depending on the season. But I've made some adjustments and have farmed out the first few hours so I can handle Mae's first diaper change of the day and breakfast. End of the day, I'll handle dinner and her bath."

Sadie did the math. That meant she'd have Mae all day. She put down the marker and turned to Drew.

"Bess will help," he said.

The man was continually reading her mind, and she wasn't certain if that was a good thing or not.

"What?" he asked as she stared at him.

Sadie quickly regrouped. "I'd like to utilize Bess for backup only. It certainly isn't fair to dump more on her." She shook her head. "Right now, having a baby in the house is a novelty. That's going to fade quickly."

"You're right, but if Mae stays at the ranch, I will need help."

Once again, reality tossed cold water on Sadie. Just when she thought an unpleasant diaper and mastering baby formulas were the most significant hurdles she'd face. She rubbed the tense muscles at the back of her neck. "I hadn't thought that far ahead, but the same is true if Mae goes to Tulsa with me."

Drew could well afford to hire a nanny, but she couldn't. Sadie swallowed past the lump in her throat, realizing that she'd need to reevaluate every aspect of her current life-style. Especially her finances.

"I nearly forgot," Drew said with a nod. "There's a very nice childcare facility managed by the Homestead Pass Community Church. Brand-new building."

Daycare? "Delia stayed home to raise Mae. I think we should honor that choice."

"Be realistic, Sadie."

"I'm only stating the facts. Delia and Jase had a plan in place for raising their daughter. Don't you think that should impact our decisions?"

"Sure. I get that. Two parents. Except that's not us."

He was right. Two singles did not a pair make.

Sadie looked away. Everything circled back to their new normal. Or not so normal.

"Let's take this one week at a time," Drew said. His voice had gentled. "That's the only way this will work."

One week. One day. One hour. Yes. That was pretty much the only way to fend off panic. She nodded and picked up a marker again. Drew would cover breakfast and dinner, and she had everything in between. It looked like she'd be getting plenty of experience. This would be training week one for her, and she'd focus on that and find a way to care for a baby and work virtually with her teaching assistant when she wasn't changing diapers.

It would be a juggling act. But women did it all the time. Her situation wasn't special or even unique. Simply new to her.

She could do this. She had to.

As she began to fill in Friday's slot, Drew cleared his throat.

"About Friday."

"Yes?" Sadie turned slowly as a frisson of dread shot through her. She'd heard that tone plenty of times before in her life. Always right before the other shoe dropped.

"I'm flying to Billings early Friday."

"Excuse me? What? Where?" He couldn't be serious.

"I'm flying to Billings. It's in Montana."

Sadie inhaled sharply. "I know where Billings is. Why are you going to Billings?"

"Business. This trip was scheduled a long time ago." He paused. "Things have been so upside down the last few days that I forgot until I got a notification on my phone."

"This Friday?" For a moment, Sadie stared at him, unable to believe that he was casually pulling the rug out from under her. "And when will you be back?"

"Sunday."

"Technically, that's when my vacation ends. What could be so important that you need to leave while we're in the middle of…." Sadie waved a hand in the air. "Of whatever this is."

"I'm speaking on a panel at a conference. Like I said. I committed long ago. My word is important to me."

"A conference. What sort of conference?" Now she was curious. Ranchers attended conferences?

"Stock Growers Association. I'm speaking on AI management in beef cattle."

"AI?" Sadie repeated, her interest piqued. "As in artificial intelligence?"

Drew laughed, then quickly worked to maintain a straight face. "Artificial insemination."

"Oh!" Heat raced up her neck. "I see."

"Do you?" Drew cocked his head. "And do you know anything about ranch life?"

"I…" She paused and released a breath. "No. I don't know anything about ranches. Or cows or whatever else it is you do here. Maybe you could tell me about a typical day."

He offered an infuriating smile. "There is no such thing as a typical day. My days start before dawn and are as long as they need to be."

She could only stare at him in stunned surprise.

"I think we should proceed on the premise that your leave will be approved," he went on. "Your supervisor wouldn't have mentioned it if she didn't think it was a sure thing. And given the fact that I'm going out of town, I think it would be a good idea for you to get to know the workings of the Lazy M."

"Why?"

"It will help you to get a better understanding of the ranch and why I believe Homestead Pass is where Mae should grow up."

Sadie mulled his response for a moment. She did say she

wanted the best for Mae. While she ached at the thought of leaving Delia's baby here, Drew had a valid point. The only way she could determine the best placement was to find out more about the ranch. "Okay."

His brow creased. "I expected you to balk."

"No. I'm trying to be objective. If the ranch is the best place for Mae, I'll be the first to admit that." Sadie paused. "Do you have any literature you'd recommend I read?"

"No books. Hands-on. Let's shoot for Tuesday for your first lesson if Mae is still improving."

"All right." Even as she said the words, Sadie knew she'd do research. Far too much of her life had been spent in situations where she had no control. The best way to avoid reliving the worst moments of her past was to be prepared. And she would be. Because there was no way she wanted to look foolish in front of Drew Morgan.

Boots in one hand and hat in the other, Drew followed the aroma of freshly brewed coffee into the kitchen.

Across the room, Sadie leaned against the counter and stared bleary-eyed at the dry-erase board he had mounted on the kitchen wall. Her dark hair had been pulled into a long braid that hung down her back. Oblivious to his presence, she sighed loudly, her expression reflecting buyer's remorse.

Drew did his best not to chuckle at the sight.

"Morning, Sadie."

"Is four a.m. considered morning?" Her gaze skipped over him before she opened a cupboard and grabbed a mug. When the last spits and wheezes of the coffee maker stopped, she filled the mug to the brim before easing into a chair.

"Around here it is," he said. Drew followed her example and poured his own mugful before lifting the foil on a plate of biscuits on the counter. "Don't forget to eat something. Lunch is a long way off.

"I'm not a breakfast person. Coffee will do."

"It's not about being a breakfast person. The body needs fuel to run from now until noon. There won't be any breaks."

She reached for a banana. "Okay, boss."

"Good morning!" Drew turned at Bess's singsong greeting. She bustled into the kitchen, tossed a copy of the *Homestead Pass Daily Journal* on the counter and shrugged out of her jacket. "All ready, are you?"

"Getting there," Drew said.

Sadie turned her head in the housekeeper's direction. "Bess. I feel terrible asking you to come in so early. I hope you don't mind."

"Honey, do I look like I'm upset?" Bess grinned. "I not only don't mind, but I'm in hog heaven. Can't wait for our girl to wake up." She nodded toward the baby monitor on the kitchen table.

"Well, I'm grateful," Sadie said.

"No problem." Bess looked to Drew. "Are you going to get Sadie on a horse?"

"Hadn't planned to."

"You want her to go back to Tulsa without a picture for her social media accounts?" the housekeeper asked.

"Um, I don't do social media," Sadie said.

"All the same, after hanging out here with these crusty old bachelors, you deserve at least a few bragging rights," Bess returned.

Crusty bachelors? Drew frowned and looked at Sadie. "Your call. I didn't think you'd want to ride a horse."

Sadie set down her mug. "What does that mean?"

"You're an academic. Said so yourself."

"That has no bearing on this topic. I feel certain I can learn to ride a horse with sufficient preparation."

His lips twitched. "You just let me know when you're... prepared."

"I'll do that," Sadie said.

Bess glanced between them, surprise flickering in her eyes. "I'm sure Sadie can do anything she sets her mind to."

"Thank you, Bess."

The housekeeper smiled and then turned. "All right, then. I'll be on my way."

"Wait. I nearly forgot," Sadie called. "I made a list for you. My phone number. The pediatrician and cardiac doctor's phone numbers. Also, the signs of distress the pediatrician mentioned." She looked around, lifting place mats and searching the tabletop. "I must have left it in my room. I'll be right back."

Bess clucked her tongue as Sadie left the room. "You know, if it were anyone but Miss Sadie, I'd be insulted by a list. But that woman goes above and beyond." She looked up at Drew. "You have to give her credit."

"Yep." Drew sipped his coffee. Dry-erase board. A dozen or so books and endless research. Above and beyond was one way to put it.

Bess narrowed her gaze. "You go easy on her out there, Drew."

He jerked his head up. "What's that supposed to mean?"

"It means you best remember that she's the one that left her comfort zone to come to Homestead Pass. She's working awfully hard to do what's best for that baby. Cut her some slack."

The housekeeper's response hit him right in his guilty conscience. "You're right, Bess."

"Of course I am."

"Here's the list," Sadie said as she raced into the kitchen. "And the pediatric cardiologist has the house phone number as a backup. Their office will call if they can get Mae in sooner."

"Got it. Thank you, sweetie." Bess put the paper on the refrigerator with a smiley face magnet. She grinned as she turned to them. "You're doing a great job, Sadie. You know that, right?"

"Am I?" Sadie's smile faltered.

"Yes. A lesser woman would have run in the other direction. Delia would be proud of you." Bess sniffed and wiped her eyes. "Now, if you'll excuse me. I really must get some chores done before our princess wakes."

"Thanks again, Bess," Sadie said.

"No problem, honey." She took two steps and stopped. "Oh, Drew, that dog is waiting on the front porch."

"Cooper?" Drew raised his brows. "Waiting for what?"

"You, I imagine." She shook her head.

Sadie grabbed her mug from the table, rinsed it out and placed it in the dishwasher before turning to him. "Anything I should know before we start?"

"First rule of ranch life. Watch where you step."

"Okay. What's the second rule?"

"Leave everything the way you found it."

"Sounds easy enough."

"If it were easy, everyone would be ranching," he replied.

Sadie offered a thoughtful nod as she picked a piece of lint from her pants.

Drew eyed her black dress slacks. Office chic wouldn't cut it in the barn or the field. "Is that what you're wearing?"

"Yes." Sadie glanced down at herself and then up at him. "Why?"

"Don't you have a pair of Wranglers?"

"Wranglers?" She frowned. "Oh, you mean jeans. No. It's not like I planned to tour a cattle ranch, or for that matter, stay in Homestead Pass."

"You didn't bring a pair of jeans with you?"

"I don't own a pair of jeans."

"I never heard of such a thing." Drew shook his head. "Guess the pants will have to do until you get to town. But what's that on your feet?"

Sadie pulled up her pant leg, displaying short black boots with a chunky two-inch heel. "They're suede booties."

"Suede? Sure hope they didn't cost too much because they'll never be the same after today."

"It will be fine."

"Don't say I didn't warn you." He continued his assessment. "You'll need a jacket."

"I'm wearing a sweater."

"You could use a sweater and a jacket. This is spring in Oklahoma. Right now, it's thirty-eight degrees. The day will start out cold. Could rain or might end up giving you a sunburn." He cocked his head. "Follow me." Drew strode to the hall closet and pulled out a puffy navy blue thermal vest. "Here you go."

She stepped back. "I stopped wearing hand-me-downs a long time ago."

"If it was good enough for my mother, it's good enough for you, don't you think?"

Sadie blinked, and her mouth formed a small circle of surprise. "Oh, I'm so sorry. I didn't mean to insult your mother."

"No need to apologize." He removed a straw cowboy hat from a hook inside the door. "Think of it as upcycling. Around here, we were upcycling before it was cool."

She slipped into the vest and placed the hat on the back

of her head before peeking at herself in the hall mirror. Her brown eyes rounded. "I look ridiculous."

"No, you don't." The fact was, despite the slightly crushed crown on the old hat, she looked kind of cute. Though he'd never say that aloud. Theirs was a business arrangement, and he never mixed business with...well, with anything else. Besides, sooner or later, Sadie would be long gone. She lived in a world far removed from a ranch in the middle of nowhere.

When she reached to withdraw the hat, Drew intercepted her hand, then quickly pulled back from the contact. "Don't take it off. You look fine."

"I feel silly," she murmured. Gaze averted, she frowned.

"Sadie, there isn't anyone on the ranch at four in the morning looking at your outfit."

"I guess that's true."

He turned back to the closet and pulled out a plastic bin.

"What are you looking for now?"

"Gloves. Ah, here they are. Don't want to ruin your manicure."

She stiffened as she accepted the leather gloves from him. "Look, I may be a city girl, but I am hardly high-maintenance."

"Good to know." He closed the closet door and faced her. "Ready to go?"

"Um, maybe I better visit the ladies' room if it's going to be such a long day."

"I'll meet you outside."

Drew grabbed two water bottles from the fridge. He hesitated, then filled a plastic bag with biscuits and tucked it into his pocket before he stepped out onto the front porch. Crisp spring air greeted him, and he inhaled deeply. There was something comforting about the smell of the ranch in the early morning. The loamy scent of earth, along with the clean air. And there was nowhere else he wanted to be.

A moment later, the soft jingle of a dog collar had him turning his head.

"Cooper. What are you doing here?"

The dog whined and rubbed his head against Drew's leg.

"Cooper, you're going to get me in trouble."

The words elicited yet another pleading whine.

Drew glanced around and pulled out the bag of biscuits. "Okay, fine. But just one, and you better not tell Gramps."

"I see your buddy is joining us." Sadie stepped out onto the porch and beneath the yellow bug light.

Drew turned and met her gaze. Sadie offered him a soft smile that gave him pause. Yeah, Bess was right. The woman was out of her comfort zone, yet she stood there on the porch, chin up, looking brave and confident in his mother's vest and a battered straw hat.

Cooper wasted no time approaching Sadie, searching for a head rub.

She hesitated before reaching to stroke the red-gold fur. After a moment, she seemed to relax.

"Ever consider that maybe Cooper is here for you?" Drew asked. "I told you, he likes you."

"Why would he like me?"

"Dogs sense your heart. They have an innate ability to know if a person is good. And once they give you a stamp of approval, they're your buddy for life. Dogs are loyal, and they'll never, ever let you down." Cooper barked as if in agreement, his dark eyes bright with enthusiasm.

"I'll remember that."

He handed her a flashlight. "Follow me. Keep an eye on the ground. This time of year, the gravel is uneven and full of mud puddles."

She matched her stride to his, which couldn't be easy as she was a good five inches shorter than his six feet. "So, we're going to do something with the cows today?"

Drew snorted. "Cattle, not cows."

"What does that mean?"

"It means that all cows are cattle, but not all cattle are cows. To answer your question, it's spring on the ranch. We have a lot of work to do. Prepping equipment, field cleanup for spring crops, fence repair and so on. And you and I have calving duty."

"Calving duty?"

"Yep. We're about to relieve Trevor and Lucas. That's why Cooper is out and about. Normally he's in his kennel until daylight."

"I'm confused. Relieve Trevor and Lucas from what?"

"Calving duty. The end of March is the middle of calving season. We keep the herd close to home this time of year, as about ten percent of our heifers need assistance delivering. Since they are no respecters of time, calving duty is round the clock."

"I see."

"No. But you will." Drew nodded toward the building in the distance. "We're headed to the barn." He moved the beam of light to illuminate a puddle. "Watch your step."

"Yes, sir."

Sadie skirted the puddle, and her attention went to the sky. "Wow, look at those stars. Everything is so clear out here."

"Yeah, I guess it is."

They walked in silence for a minute. Then Sadie pointed to the side-by-sides parked outside the barn. "You have golf carts."

"Utility vehicles."

"Is there a difference?"

"Yeah. We don't play golf here." He nodded his head to the left. "The path veers to the right now."

A moment later, the light on the main barn came into view, illuminating their route to its big open doors farther up ahead.

"A real barn," Sadie breathed.

Drew couldn't help but smile. "Yep. A real barn."

"What's that long building over there?"

"Bunkhouse."

"You have a bunkhouse?"

"A small one. Some of the crew live on the ranch when it's busy. Depends on the time of year. Mostly part-timers who move from ranch to ranch. We even take on interns from the AG program at OSU."

"No women?"

"We've had some in the past. A couple or three." The expression on Sadie's face had him raising a palm in defense. "Hey, I can't hire them if they don't apply. Finding a qualified fella or woman who wants to work on a ranch isn't easy anymore. This is a hard life. Can't say I blame them."

"Do you do the hiring?"

"Yeah. Hiring. Training and everything in between. Sam stays behind his desk and is hands-on when he gets tired of wrestling paperwork."

"What about Trevor and Lucas?"

"Trevor." Drew sighed. "You may as well know up front that Trever has had a rough road. Lost his wife a few years back. Right now, he's my right hand. Manages the stock and fills in where needed."

She nodded.

"Lucas is here off and on, depending on his bank account and his health. He's on the rodeo circuit the rest of the time, though I'm hoping he'll retire soon. We could use his expertise on the ranch."

"Rodeo?" Her eyes widened with interest.

"I said all that, and all you heard was rodeo?" Drew laughed. "Yeah, all the Morgan brothers got the rodeo itch at one time or another. Trevor did some bulldogging. That's steer wrestling. Lucas and Sam are bronc riders."

"And you?"

"Bronc rider." He heard the pride in his own voice and couldn't help a smile. His rodeo days were long gone, but they were part of the bond that tied him to ranch life.

"Sounds exciting."

"Like everything around here, it sounds much more exciting than it is in real time."

"And what's that other building over there?" she asked, gesturing to another white building in the distance.

"That's the horse barn. The stables. It empties into a fenced-in paddock."

She tipped back her head and met his gaze, her expression serious. "I meant what I said. About riding a horse."

"Is that right?"

"Yes. I'd like to schedule a time on the calendar so that I can study in preparation."

"Study? Sadie, you can't study your way through life."

"Sure you can. My life is evidence that the theory works. If I can read about a subject, I can master a subject."

"Maybe that's how things work in your world, but on the ranch, you master a task by hard work."

"Does that mean you won't let me ride?"

"I didn't say that. Get yourself a pair of Wranglers and proper boots, and we'll talk. The Hitching Post in town has everything you need."

"Yes. I'll do that." She smiled once again. "This is going to be fun."

"Let's see if you feel that way at five o'clock."

Ahead of them, Lucas stood in the doorway of the barn with a frown on his face. "About time you showed up. I'm ready to hit the sack." His gaze went to Sadie, and his eyes reflected surprise. "Miss Sadie. Good morning. Has my brother got you taking a shift too?"

"Good morning," she called. "I'm shadowing Drew."

"Got it." A grin split his brother's face. "That's some hat you've got on."

Sadie turned to Drew. "No one will be looking at my outfit, huh?"

Drew struggled to keep a straight face. "Come on. Let's find Trevor and get an update on the calving situation."

He glanced at the big clock on the wall. Oh, it was going to be a long day.

Chapter Five

Sadie wiped the sweat from her face with the edge of her shirt. Overhead, the sun beat down on her, making it difficult to recall that she had started the day in a sweater and vest.

She leaned against the front bumper of the UTV holding a wire grip for Drew as he pulled a portion of the barbed wire taut with fence pliers. Around them, the pasture had greened significantly in the last few days, and the scent of clover drifted past each time the wind danced through the trees.

"There, that ought to work." Drew gave the fence a critical assessment and then turned to her. "You should head on in. It's nearly dinnertime."

"I'll stay until you're done." At her response, every single muscle in her body cried out for her to do as Drew suggested. Sadie shook her head. No. She was determined to complete her tour of duty, even if it killed her. Sadie shuddered recalling the up-close and real calving she'd observed today. If her squeamish heart could endure that, then she'd make it a few more hours until her shift was officially over.

"Now you're just being contrary." Drew tugged off his

gloves and fished the UTV keys from his pocket before tossing the pliers into the back of the vehicle.

"I am not."

He chuckled, then pulled out a black bandana and wiped his face. "If it makes you feel any better, you impressed me today."

"I did?" She perked up at his words.

"Sure. You've been out here since four a.m. without complaining, and you've made yourself useful. I couldn't have assisted that nervous heifer with delivery without your help. I could see you were uneasy, but you overcame your fears. You ought to be proud of yourself. I have ranch hands who don't work as hard as you did today."

Sadie blinked. "I… Thank you."

"No. Thank *you*."

He whistled loudly, and Cooper came running toward them from the pasture where he'd been chasing squirrels. Sadie hadn't realized dogs could smile until today. Cooper seemed to be grinning, with his tongue lolling and his tail wagging. When Drew slid into the cab of the doorless UTV, the dog leaped into the back.

"What are you going to do next?" she asked.

"I'll check in with Trevor. I'm hoping he'll tell me that the end of calving is in sight."

"I don't understand the significance."

"We've doubled the herd size with the calves. Cattle have to eat every single day, and hay costs money. The north pasture is greening up, and grass is free. With the threat of winter storms over, we're just waiting for calving season to end so we can move the herd to grass."

"Oh, that makes sense." There was so much to ranch life that she didn't understand and every bit of it fascinated Sadie. "Shall I go with you to chat with Trevor?"

"Not necessary. Besides, Bess will have dinner in the oven and will be ready to head home."

"I nearly forgot. Bess has been here all day. You're right." She nodded. It would be thoughtless to take up more of the housekeeper's time.

Drew drove a zigzag course over the pasture trail, working to avoid the bumps with little success. Sadie's hand shot out when the vehicle swerved suddenly.

"Sorry about that," he said with a grimace. "The trails are nothing but holes this time of year from the rain."

They drove along the fence line where Drew had spent the last few hours inspecting and repairing. While he'd worked on the barbed wire and posts, Sadie had collected fallen branches and piled them into the trailer hitched to the UTV. All part of pasture maintenance, she'd learned.

For hours they'd worked together in companionable silence. In the past, she'd always preferred to tackle projects solo, but working with Drew was different. He didn't engage in idle chatter but patiently explained the workings of the ranch as though she were a peer.

As the UTV pulled up to the barn, Sadie found herself disappointed that the day was coming to a close. "Do you want help unloading the brush?" she asked.

"Nah, I'll have the crew take care of that."

"Okay, then. I guess I'll see you at dinner." Cooper barked when Sadie stepped out of the vehicle.

"Yes, ma'am." He reached out and grabbed the dog's collar. "Not you, boy. You've got supper waiting in the barn."

"Thank you for the education. I enjoyed today."

"Has it provided any revelations about the ranch as Mae's future home?"

"I'm still processing. However, I can honestly say that I would have liked to grow up on your ranch."

"Really? How's that?"

"Today, I met a chicken, a goat, horses and cows." She played with the fingers of her gloves. "I am willing to concede that a well-rounded education should include book learning and time in the field."

Drew cocked his head, his grin widening. For a moment, Sadie found herself lost in the warmth of his blue eyes. Then she looked away, horrified to realize that her heart had skittered beneath his gaze.

No. No. No. Drew Morgan was her partner in a guardianship plan. Nothing more. She wasn't even in the category of woman that a man like him would think about romantically.

She turned away quickly, all the while scolding herself. Hadn't she had enough rejection in her life? Why would she go looking for it?

"Sadie?"

"Yes?" She glanced over her shoulder.

He pushed the brim of his hat back with a finger. "I'd hire you in a heartbeat."

"Thank you," she murmured, working to hide her pleasure at the compliment.

Despite her exhaustion, her steps were light as she walked the path to the house. At the front door, she slipped off her mud-caked booties and set them to the side. Drew had been right. They were destined for the trash bin. If she wanted to ride a horse before her time in Homestead Pass was over, then the sooner she went into town to shop for essential clothing the better.

She padded down the hall to the kitchen and found Mae in her high chair and Bess at the sink. Mae squealed with delight when she saw Sadie. Okay, that was progress. Mae hadn't screwed up her face or spit up at the sight of her.

Pulling her hands from the sudsy water, Bess turned.

Her eyebrows lifted as she reached for a towel. "My word. Look at you."

A quick glance down at herself confirmed Bess's dismay. Sadie wore a fine layer of red dirt from top to bottom, along with splashes of dried mud. "I'll wash up."

Bess chuckled, her eyes sparkling with amusement. "Oh, honey, you need more than a washup. Go shower."

"I don't want to keep you."

"It's okay. I still have to frost the cake. I'm waiting for it to cool." She motioned to the counter, where a chocolate sheet cake rested in a large baking pan. "Go shower."

"Thanks, Bess."

Sadie headed down the hall to her room. She closed the door and stared at herself in the full-length mirror, stunned. Her face was dark with dust and grit, and her hair had come loose from the braid in several places. Once she removed the straw hat, dried bits of grass drifted to the ground.

No one at the college would even recognize her. She hardly recognized herself. Yet, despite her appearance and exhaustion, Sadie knew she'd gladly do it all over again. Ranch work was different than academics. The physical labor was invigorating and made her feel like she was a part of the adventure of ranch life. At the end of the day, there was a satisfaction that she could actually see and put her hands on. She liked it—a lot.

Was this the life for Mae? Her tiny apartment didn't compare.

Ten minutes later, Sadie emerged from the shower, slipped into clean clothes, braided her hair and headed back to the kitchen.

"There, now. Don't you feel better?" Bess asked.

"There is significantly less grit in my eyes and my mouth." She glanced around. "Where's Mae?"

"I put her in the play yard. She'll be fine for a bit. The monitor is on the table." Once again, Bess looked her up and down.

"What?" Sadie asked at the silent assessment.

"I can't believe you made it through the entire day." The housekeeper shook her head. "Last female I recall that kept up with the boys was their momma."

The words gave Sadie pause, and she tucked them away, knowing she'd remember today for a long time. "Has Drew come in yet?" she asked.

"No. He called and said to put the oven on warm. They ran into a little problem."

"Maybe I should help them."

"No. You sit down and relax for a minute. I'll be leaving shortly."

"Oh, yes. Of course."

The housekeeper waved an arm toward the counter. "I've got a fresh pot of coffee over there, and this seems like a good time to share a little secret."

"A secret?"

Bess opened the refrigerator, pulled out a stone crock labeled *lard* and placed it on the table. "This is my secret treat stash. Even Gus doesn't know about this jar." She opened the lid to reveal a neat stack of chocolate cookies. "Those boys pretend they're fussy eaters, but the truth is they'd eat a bowl of screwdrivers if I served them up. I have to keep a treat or two hidden for myself."

Sadie laughed at the comment and eyed the plump chocolate cookies with macadamia nuts and white chips.

"Now, help yourself to a cookie and have a nice cup of coffee while you wait on the menfolk for dinner." Bess poured coffee into two mugs and slipped into a chair across from Sadie.

"I appreciate this, Bess." She pulled out a cookie and worked to relax.

"How'd you like your day on the ranch?"

"I loved it!" The enthusiastic response was out of her mouth before Sadie could rein it back in. But she had no regrets. After all, this was a once-in-a-lifetime experience. She'd seen cattle birth and participated in the camaraderie of the ranch crew as they worked steadily from sunrise to near sunset. She had a new appreciation for the Lazy M Ranch and for herself. Maybe it was pure stubbornness kept her going, but Bess was right, she ought to pat herself on the back for today.

"Is that so?" Bess offered a thoughtful nod. "I meant what I said. Can't say I've seen another woman spend the entire day like you did since the missus was alive."

"Drew said he'd hired women for the crew in the past."

"Those gals don't count. Mostly buckle bunnies. They only hired on because the Morgan boys are so handsome. Didn't ever last long, I can tell you that. Not that there aren't some experienced cowgirls out there. There are. But the ones I know work on their family land or are out on the circuit."

"The circuit?"

"The rodeo."

Sadie sipped the rich, strong coffee that made what she brewed at home seem like bathwater in comparison. "Oh, yes. Drew mentioned the rodeo."

"Did he mention getting you on a horse?"

"We're going to schedule that. That is, if my family-leave paperwork is approved."

"When will you find out?"

"I hope I know by the time Drew returns from his trip on Sunday."

"If it turns out you get to stay, I've got an idea." She grinned and raised her brows. "Just between us gals."

"Okay." Sadie said the word slowly while she studied the housekeeper, whose eyes danced with mirth.

"You do your book learning on how to ride a horse, and how about if I give you a riding lesson?"

"How will you do that without Drew finding out? If he does, I'll be eating 'I told you so' for breakfast, lunch and dinner."

Bess slapped her thigh and burst out laughing. "See, there. I knew you were my kind of gal."

"I like to think I'm open-minded when it comes to pulling the wool over Drew's eyes." Sadie bit back her own laugh.

"You're open-minded, and I have a horse." Bess crossed her arms and leaned back in the chair, slowly nodding her head.

"You do?"

"Yep, and she's as sweet as can be. Perfect for beginners. She's the last horse left on my farm."

"You have a farm too?"

"I lease out the land. But there's enough acreage surrounding the house to plant a disreputable vegetable garden and for a few chickens to cause trouble."

"And your horse?"

"Sweet Pea has her own stables, and I try to ride daily."

"Sweet Pea? I love that name."

"She's a pretty chestnut mare that my husband bought for me. Bless his soul. The hubby's been with the Lord a good long time now, but Sweet Pea is a reminder of how much he loved me."

"Oh, Bess. I'm so sorry for your loss."

"Thank you." Bess sipped her coffee and then glanced around before leaning closer. "So, what do you think?"

She lowered her voice. "No one else has to know about this. Those boys sure can't keep a secret. You best remember that."

This time Sadie couldn't resist laughing. "I can hardly wait."

"That's how I feel about seeing the look on Drew's face when he sees you saddle and ride one of the Lazy M horses all by yourself."

Sadie considered the plan. Good-natured fun. Why not? She, too, leaned closer. "We'll have to tell him eventually, won't we?"

"Absolutely. However, it's been my experience that *eventually* has a very long shelf life."

Laughter slipped from Sadie's lips. "Oh, Bess. I am so fortunate to have met you."

"I feel the same, honey. You're like the daughter I never had."

Sadie smiled at Bess's precious words. Words she had waited her entire life to hear.

"Bess, that was so much fun." Sadie held a pastry box filled with cannoli as they exited the inn on Thursday evening.

"Nice to make something that isn't industrial-sized. I get mighty weary of the Texas sheet cakes and the endless chocolate chip cookies I feed the boys." She grinned. "And I'm so pleased that Chef Moretti convinced you to participate. It's much more fun than observing."

Yes, participating was more fun than observing, and wasn't that sort of Drew's mantra for her? She was beginning to realize that taking chances wasn't as frightening as it had been as an orphan living in a group home with Delia so many years ago.

"Yoo-hoo! Bess!"

Both Sadie and Bess whirled around at the voice calling the housekeeper.

A bubbly brunette in tight black jeans, red cowboy boots and a denim shirt approached them, smiling.

"Olivia." Bess grinned as she hugged the woman.

Olivia pushed her oversize sunglasses to the top of her head and laughed. "It's so good to see you."

"You too. This is such a surprise. What are you doing in town?"

"I'm back for my daddy's birthday. The big six-o."

"How long are you here?"

"Not long. I'm trying to stay under the radar." She glanced up and down the street and raised her brows meaningfully. "You never saw me."

Sadie looked between the two. Clearly, Bess and Olivia had a long history.

Bess grabbed Sadie's hand and pulled her close. "Olivia Moretti, this is Dr. Sadie Ross. She's staying at the ranch. Friend of Drew's."

"Oh?" The brunette's eyes rounded with unabashed surprise.

"No. No," Sadie quickly responded. "Nothing like that. I'm visiting. I'm a college professor from Tulsa."

"Well, that's too bad. You look like you could handle our Drew." She smiled and held out a hand. "Liv Moretti. I grew up in Homestead Pass, though I spend most of my time on the road now, consulting."

Sadie took the other woman's hand. Her grip was firm, and the dark eyes were welcoming. "Nice to meet you. You're related to Chef Moretti?"

"Yes. My aunt Loretta. Actually, I'm Chef Moretti as well."

"That's quite a family legacy," Sadie said. She was always both curious and in awe of multiple generations of families, like the Morettis and Morgans, since she had no family tree.

"It really is. Sometimes it can be a bit overwhelming." Liv glanced at her watch and then looked to Bess. "I have to dash, but I'll call you and give you an update on the family."

"You had better."

"Hope to see you again, Sadie," Liv said with a friendly grin.

Sadie gave Liv a wave as the woman moved down the street and out of sight as quickly as she had appeared.

"I gather there is a connection between Liv and the Morgans," Sadie said.

Bess nodded toward the parking lot. "Come on, let's head to the cars. Too many ears around here." When they turned the corner, she glanced around as if to be sure they were alone. "Olivia and Sam were engaged once upon a time. She broke up with him a week before the wedding."

"Sam." *Not Drew.* Why did she feel relief?

"Childhood sweethearts they were."

Sadie nodded as Bess continued.

"I'd tell you what happened, but I'm not sure myself. I don't think anyone has been privy to what happened. It's been four years, and I know as much now as then. And while I like information as much as the next person, I don't pry in matters of the heart." She paused. "Probably best not to mention we saw Olivia. No need to stir the hornet's nest. Sam's mighty sensitive about the subject."

"Of course," Sadie said. "Um, is there anything I should know about Drew?" She swallowed, heat rushing to her face. "I mean, I don't want to accidentally say something awkward regarding his...personal life."

"Drew?" She scoffed. "I don't think the man has ever

been in a serious relationship, come to think about it. He tends to find himself in hopeless situations."

"What does that mean?"

"Gets himself into relationships that are doomed from the get-go." Bess shook her head. "I'm not a psychiatrist, but if I were to speculate, I'd say that boy has boot-drop sickness."

"Excuse me?"

"If you find yourself tangled up with someone with whom there is no future, you don't ever have to worry about the other boot dropping." Bess shook her head.

"Why would he do that?"

"The loss of his parents, maybe." She shrugged. "Then again. What do I know?"

Sadie frowned. Drew seemed so decisive about everything. She didn't know what to think about Bess's summary, though it probably wasn't any of her business. After all, she was leaving Homestead Pass soon.

"We best hurry home," Bess said with a glance up at the sky.

The woman was right. The skies opened as they left town—Sadie for the ranch and Bess for her house. When Sadie arrived, she pulled out her umbrella and dodged puddles as she ran from her car to the front steps while another round of thunder and lightning began.

Just as she was about to open the front door, it swung open and Drew appeared. Sadie began to pitch forward, but a warm hand on her arm steadied her.

"Careful there."

She stared up into his blue eyes and worked to engage her brain. "I, ah… I wasn't expecting that."

"I saw you pull up from the kitchen window."

"Thank you."

"How'd cooking school go?"

"It was fun." She held up the pastry box as she slipped off her wet shoes. "Cannoli." She narrowed her gaze. "Don't you leave early tomorrow?"

"Yeah, but I wanted a minute to review things with you." He headed into the kitchen, and she followed. "Want some coffee?"

"No thanks. I'm good."

He nodded and poured himself a cup. "I just wanted to make sure you're comfortable with everything while I'm gone. See if you have any questions or concerns."

"I don't think so. Do you?" She paused. "Are you worried I can't handle Mae on my own?"

"No. Of course not. But Bess won't be here on Saturday."

"I won't oversleep if that's what concerns you. And Gus and I already decided that we'd order pizza for Saturday night dinner, as long as I agreed to jalapeños on half the pizza. His half."

"I'm not concerned, Sadie."

She frowned when he leaned against the counter and crossed his arms. It would be helpful if the man looked less larger-than-life. She didn't get it. Jeans and a denim shirt. That was all that set him apart from other men. And that ridiculous dimple when he smiled. Yet, it seemed like the other men she'd met failed to measure up to this one. It made no sense, and she wasn't pleased about the revelation.

"Are you okay?" Drew asked. "I wasn't trying to insult you." He uncrossed his arms and raised a palm. "Sadie, the truth is, I feel guilty about dumping this on you."

"It's going to be fine," she assured him. "I've been doing on-the-job training for this all week."

Saying the words made Sadie realize how true they were. She was much less anxious about him leaving than she had been when he first announced the trip.

"Promise you'll call me if you run into any problems?"

"I will. Absolutely."

"Thank you. And thanks for taking this on."

"Like I said, it's going to be fine."

"Just fine." Sadie murmured the words the next morning as she put down the phone and sank into the chair next to Mae.

As if in response, Mae slapped at the tray of her high chair and offered a few syllables.

"Mae, we've got a problem."

The conversation delighted Mae, and she babbled on.

"Bess is sick. I'll need to make lunch for the crew today." Sadie sighed. "And dinner for Gus and Drew's brothers tonight." Bess was normally here on Fridays to take care of those things. Now Sadie would have to.

Mae laughed and picked up another piece of mashed banana.

"We can figure this out. Can't we, Mae?"

At the words, Mae's rubber chew animal sailed through the air and landed across the room.

"Okay, that's not helpful." Sadie reached for the latest self-help book she'd been reading this morning. She thumbed through the pages. "It says here that we should focus on what we can do instead of what we can't. Act like the situation is under control and soon it will be."

"Are you talking to yourself?"

Sadie turned to see Drew standing in the doorway with a small duffel and a briefcase. He scooped up the baby toy and placed it on the kitchen table.

"Girl talk."

"Ah." He glanced at the book in her hand. "What are you reading?"

"I picked up the latest bestseller at the bookstore."

He nodded. "So, everything is okay?"

"Everything is fine, Drew," she said brightly. "Go. Have a great conference. Mae and I have everything under control."

"What about your classes?"

"My teaching assistant has everything covered during the day, and I'm going to work on lesson plans and grading in the evening when Mae goes to sleep."

He glanced around. "Where is Bess, anyhow?"

Sadie froze, her mind scrambling. "There was a long grocery list on the refrigerator. It's gone, so maybe she stopped at the store on the way in."

"Yeah, probably so."

There was no reason to alarm Drew or force him to cancel his trip. She could handle Bess's duties. It might mean peanut butter and jelly or avocado toast, but no one would starve. They might not be happy, but they wouldn't starve.

"I printed out everyone's cell phone number," Drew said. He handed her the paper.

She looked at him and then down at the list. This was something she'd do, and she was impressed at the gesture. "Wonderful. Very helpful."

"And I put Mae's car seat in your vehicle."

"Oh, I hadn't thought of that. Thank you." She would need the car seat when they went into town with Bess's grocery list.

"No problem." Drew glanced around. "I guess that's everything."

"Sounds like it."

"I'll be back on Sunday." He looked at her. "I know this is a lot."

You have no idea.

"It's good practice," Sadie said. "After all, I asked for a chance to prove I can handle guardianship."

"Handle is one thing. This is putting your feet to the flame."

"No, it isn't. Your entire family is here if I need assistance."

"I guess you're right. Maybe I'm nervous about leaving Mae."

"She's in good hands. Trust me."

His eyes searched her face, then they connected with hers. "I do trust you, Sadie."

Her heart clutched at the softly spoken words, and she swallowed hard.

Drew leaned down to kiss Mae on the top of her head and then turned to Sadie.

She met his gaze. Should they shake hands or what? Sadie took an awkward step toward him and thrust out her hand. "Have a good trip."

"I, um, okay, then." He shook her hand, then quickly released her and backed away. "See you on Sunday."

The situation was laughable. Except for the part where Drew was leaving and Bess was home sick.

Should I walk him to the door? No, that would be even more awkward. She offered him a friendly toodle-oo wave of her fingers and began to clean up Mae's breakfast. Minutes later, the sound of gravel crunching indicated Drew had backed up his truck and left.

Sadie took a slow look around the kitchen. She was in charge. This was her kingdom for now.

What would it be like to have a home of her own like this? A family. For a brief moment, she allowed herself to dream. Then she opened a drawer and reached for a pen and paper. Enough dreaming. What she needed was a plan.

She knew there was meat in the freezer. She went to the big standing freezer and opened the door. Packaged meat and poultry from the butcher. What could she do with it, and how would she defrost a package in time for lunch?

The house phone rang, and she slammed the freezer shut and reached for the receiver. "Lazy M Ranch, Sadie speaking."

"Sadie, this is Liv Moretti. We met last night."

"Hi. Bess isn't here."

"Yes. I know. She called me. Unfortunately, she didn't have your cell phone number."

"Oh? Can I help you with something?"

"I'm calling to help you. However, once again, I must ask for your discretion. Please don't tell Sam or or any of the Morgans that I'm in town. Those boys chatter like magpies. If Sam found out, things would be all sorts of awkward."

Awkward. Well, Sadie certainly had more than a passing familiarity with that term. "You have my word, Olivia."

"Thank you. Now, let's talk about lunch and dinner."

Sadie sagged against the kitchen counter in relief. She couldn't believe what she was hearing. If this wasn't a God thing, she didn't know what it was. "Wait. You're going to help me with meal prep?"

"That's what I'm here for."

"Oh my. That seems like a big ask."

"Sadie, if Bess hasn't mentioned it, out here, womenfolk stick together. My daddy not only manages a guest ranch, but he runs four hundred head of cattle. I understand what you're up against. You do not want to show up at noon without proper sustenance for cranky and tired cowboys."

"I don't understand. How can you help?"

"I'm working on lunch right now. I'll give you directions to Homestead Pass Guest Ranch. All you have to do is stop by and pick it up."

"What?"

"I'm making lunch."

"Are you sure?"

"Very sure. This is my day job. I cook, and I'm a restaurant consultant. Cooking is like breathing for me. Besides, you'd be doing me a favor, testing a recipe on the ranch crew."

"I can't believe you're offering to do this."

"You're Bess's friend and I'm Bess's friend. That makes us pals by default. Bess has been a blessing to me since my momma passed. I owe her, and I'm happy to help." She laughed. "Who knows, I may need you to return the favor someday."

It took Sadie a moment to process Liv's response. She wasn't accustomed to such blanket generosity.

"I'm not sure I understand that rationale," Sadie said. "But you don't have to offer twice. I'll give you my cell phone number, and you can text me directions."

"Be sure to bring that baby with you when you come. I want to meet the famous Miss Mae."

"I'll do that." Sadie paused. "Did Bess say how she's doing? She sounded pretty rough when she called me earlier."

"A little stomach bug, but she didn't want to pass it along to the baby."

"I'll be praying for her," Sadie said.

"As will I. And I'll drop off a batch of soup to her house," Liv said.

"That's a great idea."

"Bess said you make a banging lasagna. So, it's lasagna for the Morgan dinner menu tonight."

A small knot formed in Sadie's stomach. "But I've only made it once and that was with Beth."

"Don't worry. I've got you covered. I'll call in a grocery order in your name and have it billed to the ranch.

All you have to do is pick it up at Green Apple Grocery in about an hour. I suggest two casseroles. I'll talk you through the prep on the phone. Then stop by my daddy's ranch around ten a.m. and I'll have dessert ready to go, along with lunch."

And just like that, the tension in her began to unfurl. "I can do that. Though I feel terrible putting this load on you."

"Honest. It's not a big deal."

After exchanging information, Sadie set down the phone and looked at Mae. "We're going shopping."

"You are?" Gus walked into the room, tugging on a pair of leather work gloves.

"Bess is ill, and I'm in charge of lunch and dinner."

He stopped in his tracks, brows raised and jaw slack. "You are?"

"Gus, you're repeating yourself." Sadie wiped off the high-chair tray with a sponge. "Don't worry. I have the situation under control." She nearly laughed aloud at the words that were nearly verbatim from the self-help book she'd been reading.

"Can you cook?"

"I guess you're about to find out," she returned.

"I sure hope that means yes. Trevor said I've got to pitch in today, and I'm going to be mighty hungry come noon." He glanced around. "What is for lunch, anyhow?"

"It's a surprise."

"I'm not a fan of surprises." Gus frowned. "Maybe I should stay and help you. Doesn't seem fair for you to have to handle everything yourself."

"Trust me. Everything is under control. You won't miss a meal."

"If you say so. My cell phone number is right there next to the landline. Call if you need me."

"I will. Thanks, Gus."

"No, ma'am, I'm not just spitting in the wind. I mean it. It would be a hardship to leave those ranch chores." He shook his head slowly. "But that's a risk I'm willing to take. You and little Miss Mae are my first priority."

She bit back a chuckle. "You're a saint, Gus."

"Aw, you're only saying that 'cause it's true." He laughed, amused by his own joke, as he headed out of the kitchen.

When he left, Sadie leaned over the kitchen sink and peered out the window. She waited a beat until he had crossed the yard and disappeared into the barn. Then she turned to Mae.

"Young lady, you and I are on a mission, and you are sworn to secrecy."

Mae chortled with delight and slapped her hand on the high-chair tray.

"Shh. Remember. It's a secret."

Sadie said a silent prayer. *Help me pull this off, Lord. I need to prove to Drew and myself that I can handle being Mae's guardian even when the rug gets pulled out from under me.*

Drew stretched his left leg into the aisle of the small plane and rolled his neck. A quick glance at his phone confirmed that he'd be back in Homestead Pass around dusk. Didn't matter if it was midnight. After a weekend away, he was ready for home.

Twice, between workshops at the conference, he'd called Sadie and gotten voice mail, which only frustrated him. He was hesitant to call a third time, lest it appear that he was checking in because he didn't trust her.

His head told him that he trusted her one hundred percent. His heart whispered that it would be nice to hear her voice and Mae's giggles.

Instead of calling Sadie again, he decided to pester

Gramps. His grandfather picked up, said he was busier than a squirrel in a nut factory and passed the phone to Trevor.

"Sadie is doing fine. She made lunch for the crew," his brother said. "Her lasagna is right up there with Bess's. Plus, she made pie for dessert. Haven't had a cherry pie that good since Liv used to drop them off for Sam."

Sadie made the crew lunch? "Wait a minute. What happened to Bess?"

"She's got that bug that's going around."

So Sadie had stepped in. They'd never really talked about her skills in the kitchen. Except for her strong opinions about foster care, there was a lot about Sadie he didn't know. She seemed to dodge questions about her past and her present, for that matter.

Though books were her lifeline, the woman wasn't exactly an open book. Some irony there.

Drew spoke to Trevor a few minutes more and hung up.

He leaned back in his seat. So, she'd made lunch for all the ranch hands while taking care of Mae. Once again, he was impressed. With each passing day, he'd begun to consider that perhaps Sadie was the better choice for Mae's guardian. Maybe he was being selfish. Sure, there was family here on the ranch. But except for Bess, they were all guys.

A little girl needed a momma, didn't she?

Drew stared down at the photo on his phone again.

He couldn't explain what he felt as he looked at the picture. Didn't dare because it made no sense. Admitting to his growing attraction and admiration for the woman was a dead-end street leading nowhere.

Sadie Ross was a thorn in his side only a week ago. What had changed?

"Is that your family?"

Drew looked up from his phone to meet the smiling face of the elderly man seated next to him on the small plane.

"I couldn't help but notice that picture on your phone. That's a beautiful family. You are surely blessed."

Drew hesitated for only a beat. "Thank you." Yeah, they were, after all, a family. If only a temporary family. And he was blessed beyond measure.

"How old is your baby?"

"Mae is six months old."

"She's mighty pretty. So is your wife."

"They are." The words slipped out easily. There was no denying the truth. Mae was the prettiest baby he'd ever seen, and though she tried to hide herself, he'd come to discover that Sadie Ross was a beautiful woman, inside and out.

Drew's aisle companion pulled out a worn leather wallet and flipped it open to a black-and-white photo of a bride and groom. "Sixty years together. She's with the Lord now. Miss her every day."

"I'm sorry for your loss, but sixty years. That's wonderful."

"It is. I pray for sixty or more for you, young man."

"Thank you, sir." Drew couldn't help but smile. Sixty years with one woman seemed a stretch when he hadn't even been on a date in a year or so.

Then his thoughts drifted to Sadie. They were a lot alike, both tied to the past by a thread they couldn't seem to cut. The death of his parents seemed an obstacle he hadn't been able to put aside.

Maybe it was that kindred spirit that drew him to her—that and her stubbornness, determination, and yeah, her beauty. She was beautiful, though she didn't have a clue. He suspected deep down, she thought she was still that awkward child no one wanted.

Maybe he ought to start showing her that wasn't true anymore. After all, they were friends now. And a real friend would do that.

Once the plane landed, Drew wasted no time grabbing his belongings and slipping through the sliding glass doors into the humid night to find his truck.

The house was dark when he pulled up, except for a light in the kitchen. Once he got out of his truck, and his eyes adjusted to the dark, Drew realized his grandfather was sitting on a porch rocker.

"Gramps, what are you doing out here?"

"Sitting. Sometimes I just like to smell the air and listen to the cows."

The gravel crunched beneath Drew's boots as he walked up to the house. He took the steps two at a time. "Why are the lights out?"

"It's been raining. Those skeeters know I'm a sweet treat, so I thought I'd outsmart them."

Drew grinned, leaning against the rail. It was good to be home. Except for the lowing of cattle, the night was still. "Sure is quiet tonight."

"Just the way I like it."

"Sadie awake?"

"Last I checked, she was in the nursery watching Mae sleep."

"Watching Mae sleep… Is the baby all right?"

"A little fussy tonight, that's all. Don't get yourself all excited. Babies get fussy sometimes, you know."

"No. I don't."

"Trust me. They do." Gramps grinned. "How was your trip?"

"Good. Good." His gaze spanned the land before him, taking in the dark shadows of the barn and the tree line in the distance. "I remember when I thought I wanted to see the world," he murmured. "Now I get antsy and want to get home after twenty-four hours."

"I hear you."

"Funny, how your priorities change as you get older."

His grandfather snorted. "Tell me about it."

"You know, Gramps. A fella on the plane told me he'd been married sixty years. Imagine that."

"That surprise you? You know, your grandmother and I were married forty years before I lost her. And your parents, why, they met when they were in grade school. That means they were together for more than thirty years."

"Thirty, forty years." He let out a rush of air. "That's a long time."

"Not when you spend those years with your best friend."

Silence stretched between them as Drew considered his grandfather's words.

"What are you afraid of, son?"

"Huh…what?" Drew jerked back. "I'm not afraid."

"Seems to me like you are. You're either afraid of picking the wrong one or that she'll be snatched away too soon like your folks."

Drew hesitated before answering. Then realized there was no use protesting. The senior Morgan had cultivated a strong baloney radar over the years. Instead, Drew simply nodded and pushed away from the railing. "You could be right."

"You going in?" his grandfather asked.

"Yeah." Drew picked up his duffel and briefcase.

"I'll be in shortly as well."

Light from the nursery reflected into the hallway. Drew left his bag in the foyer and slipped off his boots. He padded toward the nursery and peeked his head in.

Mae lay on her tummy, babbling quietly and playing with her fingers. He kept out of sight so she wouldn't see him and wake Sadie, who slept in the rocking chair across from the crib. She'd have a neck crick in the morning. Should he wake her? No. The rhythmic rise and fall of her chest told him she was in a deep slumber.

As she slept beneath the glow of the nursery lamp, Drew could see a scattering of freckles on the bridge of her nose. He'd never noticed the freckles before. Nor had he noticed how long her eyelashes were as they rested on her cheeks.

After only a week, he found himself noticing a lot of things about Sadie. Like how she fit in on the Lazy M as though she belonged. Sure, she was a city girl, yet in his experience, she wasn't like any other city girl he'd met before. She never once hesitated to do what needed to be done. Didn't balk at getting dirty and pitching in either.

And when it came to Mae, there was nothing Sadie wouldn't do or learn to give her friend's child all the love and attention she deserved.

That alone gave him pause and had him again thinking about guardianship.

The appointment with the pediatric cardiologist was Wednesday. The outcome of that visit would impact their decisions regarding the future.

He could only pray that he was prepared for those decisions when the time came.

Chapter Six

Monday morning, Sadie walked into the kitchen with Mae and found Bess at the kitchen counter, whipping something in a bowl and belting out a tune. "This is the day that the Lord has made. So, you can be sure I'm gonna rejoice and be happy."

"Bess! You must be feeling better. What version of the Bible is that verse?"

"The Bess Lowder version, of course." The housekeeper whirled around, a smile on her face. "And yes, I am feeling much better, thank you. Your prayers were felt! Nasty bug. However, the upside is that my blue jeans are no longer snug."

Sadie carefully placed Mae in her high chair before she went to the coffee maker and poured herself a mugful of the brew. "I'm so glad, and I hear you on the pants. I usually only eat two meals a day at home, but here? Well, it's difficult to resist your cooking."

"Glad to hear that," Bess said.

Sadie glanced at the wrought iron wall clock. "You're here early."

"There's a story behind my early arrival. Generally, if I

take a day off, I come back to find things are..." She grimaced. "How shall I put it? Out of control at the ranch."

"I hope that wasn't what you found this morning." Sadie's gaze spanned the kitchen, from the clean countertops to the kitchen table. Nothing seemed amiss. She'd worked very hard to keep the place tidy, including washing several loads of clothes and towels.

"Imagine my surprise to find this place looking like I'd been here." Bess chuckled. "Things were so spick-and-span that I didn't have a choice except to make a cinnamon streusel coffee cake. It's cooling, and I'm finishing up the icing."

Sadie smiled, relieved that her efforts were appreciated.

A moment later, Drew strolled into the room, grinning. "There's my breakfast date."

"Which one of us are you talking to?" Bess asked.

"Every single one of you beautiful women."

"Good answer." Bess chuckled. "That'll get you coffee cake."

"Welcome back," Sadie said. "I'm sorry I couldn't pick up when you called. Things were busy here."

"So I heard. And thanks. Good to be home."

He smiled, and Sadie's pulse quickened. She'd missed him. The realization took her by surprise. Missed talking to him, missed watching him with Mae, and missed his smiles and quick humor. Her brain gave her heart a swift reprimand. No. The only way she'd escape this situation in one piece was to keep her guard up. Her heart offered a mocking laugh.

"You okay, Sadie?" Drew asked.

"Yes. Just thinking."

Drew nodded. "What about you, Bess? Feeling better?"

"Who told you I was under the weather?"

"I talked to Gramps." Drew's gaze moved to Sadie. "He said Sadie was superwoman in your absence."

"Pretty much," Bess said. "Though I never doubted for a moment that she could handle things."

Sadie's face warmed at the discussion. She wasn't accustomed to high praise.

"And she fed the crew?" He opened the cupboard and pulled out the baby oatmeal. "Staring down half a dozen hungry cowboys. How about that?"

"Hello? I'm right here," Sadie said. "And you don't have to sound so surprised."

Drew turned to her with his brows raised. "Do I sound surprised? Nah. That tone you hear is me being impressed." He shrugged. "Didn't even know you could cook."

Sadie shot a quick glance toward Bess. "I had help from my friends."

"Didn't know you had…." Drew stopped short as a soft gasp slipped from Sadie's mouth.

"Yes, you best stop talking," Bess said. "You just put one boot in your mouth. Fitting both of them in there won't do you any favors."

"I meant to say that I didn't know Sadie had made new friends in Homestead Pass. After all, we do keep her pretty much stuck at the ranch."

"Uh-huh." Bess raised a brow. "Nice save."

"I have friends." Sadie scrambled to defend herself without giving away Liv Moretti's identity. "Mrs. Pickett at the bookstore. Chef Moretti no cooking class. Mary McAfee at Homestead Inn." She paused. "Oh, and the pastor's wife asked me for my lasagna recipe at church yesterday and invited me to join the ladies' outreach group."

"How nice, Sadie. What did you tell Mrs. McGuinness?" Bess asked.

"I told her that recipe was Chef Moretti's and that I was only in town temporarily. So, you see, I do have friends."

Drew straddled a chair in front of Mae and stirred the oatmeal. "Montana sure is pretty this time of year."

Sadie couldn't help herself from laughing at the nervous expression on his face.

"Did you get out of the hotel at all?" Bess asked.

Drew offered Mae a spoonful of her breakfast. "Yeah. I took a quick tour of one of the operations. Huge. Over one hundred thousand acres and three thousand head of cattle. They manage the cattle by helicopter."

"Imagine that," Bess said. "A helicopter."

He nodded. "Makes me realize how the Lazy M is just a mom-and-pop operation."

"You were invited to speak at the conference," Sadie said. "That means your work on Lazy M must be well noted by your peers."

He grinned. "Did you just compliment me?"

Sadie busied herself with the morning paper so he wouldn't notice her face pinking. "Merely an observation."

"Are you looking to expand the Lazy M?" Bess asked.

"Hard to say. I'd like to keep the Lazy M as a family business. In order to expand, we'd need more family. I don't see that happening anytime soon. We've been five bachelors for the last twenty years."

"Lost cause," Bess mumbled.

"I heard that." He offered Mae another spoonful of food, and the infant turned her head, refusing to open her mouth. "Our girl is fussy this morning."

"Mae's sick?" Bess dropped the whisk and rushed to the high chair.

"I checked her temperature this morning," Sadie said. "It's normal, but she was fussing on and off last evening."

"Awfully drooly, isn't she?" The housekeeper slipped a finger into the baby's mouth and laughed.

"What's so funny?" Drew asked.

"Mae is cutting her first teeth."

"Cutting teeth?" Sadie asked.

"Yes. Wash your hands, and I'll show you."

Sadie complied and then followed Bess's instructions, rubbing her finger over Mae's lower incisor area. "Bumps."

"Notice how she likes having her gums rubbed? This little girl is teething. Those teeth will erupt anytime now."

"Teething," Sadie said. "I should have figured that out. I read about it."

"Honey, I have never met a first-time momma who has it all figured out, no matter how many books she reads."

First-time momma. No matter how many times she heard Bess refer to her as a mother, the word stopped her.

"Now that we have the diagnosis, what's the treatment?" Drew asked.

"Teething toys. Several. That way, you can always have one in the freezer chilling."

"Teething toys?" Drew asked.

Sadie looked at him. "Did you know about this?"

"It's all news to me," he admitted. "But I'm happy to drive into town this morning."

"I can do it," she said. "I have boots to pick up."

"Boots?" Drew looked at her. "You special ordered boots?"

"You told me to get boots and a hat and jeans. Mae and I went into town on Saturday and stopped at the Hitching Post."

Bess gave Drew a stern look. "Since she's getting herself all cowgirled, isn't it about time you took Sadie for a riding lesson, Drew? How about tomorrow?"

"There's no rush," Sadie said. She hadn't even begun studying yet.

He turned to Sadie. "You didn't say if your leave was approved."

"I received an email notifying me of approval on Friday. Things have been so busy, I forgot."

"Approved." Drew nodded. "That's great, but what does it mean?"

"It means I'll stay as long as I'm needed. That will depend on the cardiology appointment on Wednesday."

Drew's expression turned thoughtful. "I guess we better get your ride in quickly, then. Tomorrow work for you?"

"Absolutely. She's ready and eager," Bess said.

Sadie blinked. What? No, she wasn't ready!

"Tomorrow at two, then," Drew said.

Tomorrow? She wouldn't be prepared by tomorrow. "I, um—"

"Which horse are you getting her on?" Bess interrupted.

"Silver." Drew's cell phone rang, and he stood and accepted the call. "Yeah, sure. Give me a minute." He turned to Sadie. "I hate to dump on you again, but my presence is requested in the barn. Could you finish up with Mae?"

"No problem." She moved to the chair Drew vacated and waited for him to leave the room before she panicked. "I can't do this, Bess."

"I can feed her if you like."

"No. I'm talking about horseback riding with Drew. I haven't even had a lesson with Sweet Pea yet."

"That's why I said tomorrow."

"You and me and Mae are going to have a girls' day out. We'll pick up your boots in town and then mosey on over to my farm for a lesson."

"Today?"

"Sure. We can bring the baby monitor. We can let baby

girl gnaw on some chilled teething toys and give her a little acetaminophen when she goes down for her nap. She'll be fine. Fussy, but fine."

"What if I'm terrible?"

"Horseback riding is like changing diapers. You used to be all thumbs changing Mae's diaper. Now that you've changed about three hundred, it's no longer a big deal." She smiled. "That's how horseback riding is. You can expect to start off a bit awkward, and then you'll get better."

That did make sense… "I hope you're right."

"I am. Besides, the horse Drew is putting you on is as gentle and patient as can be. Oh, and a little insider tip. She likes peppermints. Give her a peppermint, and she'll follow you anywhere."

"If you say so."

"Now, Sadie, horses can sense your emotions. They're very empathic. Relax, and Silver will too. Show a horse you trust her, and she'll trust you."

Sadie nodded while committing Bess's words to memory. Relaxing was key. Hitting the books again couldn't hurt either.

And praying. She better be prayed up because riding a horse while Drew Morgan observed was going to be her biggest challenge yet.

"Drew, you got a minute?" Trevor called.

"Can't say that I do." Drew stepped out of the barn and headed toward the stables.

"It's Tuesday. You don't have anything scheduled. I checked."

"I forgot to put it on the team calendar. I've got an appointment in about five minutes. Can it wait?"

"An appointment doing what?"

Though Drew picked up his pace, hoping to discourage

his brother, Trevor's long legs matched his stride, kicking up dirt as he did.

"An appointment teaching Sadie to ride."

"You're taking this parenting thing kinda literally, aren't you?"

"Parenting? This has nothing to do with Mae. Sadie wants to ride, and I volunteered." He stopped abruptly and stared at his brother. "And what do you mean, 'this parenting thing'? I'm Mae's guardian."

"Not yet, you aren't."

He searched his brother's face. Something was on Trevor's mind, and there'd be no peace until he let him talk. Drew took a deep breath. "Just get there, would you?"

"Bro, you manage Lazy M. Been doing it since I was a kid. We all look up to you. But lately, something's been off. You're missing in action more than not. When you do show up, your head is somewhere else. I'm worried about you."

Drew blinked, more than a little surprised. "I appreciate the concern, but I don't see that there's a problem."

"No? Where were you this morning?"

"I had to drive to Elk City."

"Yeah, and we were supposed to have a meeting. A meeting you scheduled to discuss spring vaccination and branding."

"We can do it tomorrow. Mae had a problem." He omitted the fact that he'd driven to the nearest big town for a chew toy because Sadie couldn't find one in Homestead Pass yesterday. That information probably would not help his case.

"And what about last week? The budget meeting with Sam?"

"Was that last week?" Drew grimaced. Yeah, it was the day after he'd brought Sadie and Mae to the ranch.

"Yeah, and you forgot to place the feed order." Trevor raised his brows. "That's not like you."

A sinking feeling settled in Drew's gut as he eyed his brother. He recalled that more than a few times recently he'd had to adjust his schedule to accommodate Mae or Sadie. Was it more than likely that a few things might have been overlooked? Yeah.

Trevor was right.

"Okay," Drew returned. "Let's say your thoughts have merit."

His brother blew a raspberry and rolled his eyes.

"What do you expect me to do?" Drew asked. "I'm between a rock and a hard place."

"Look, I know that the whole Sadie and Mae thing was just dropped on you, and I get that you're honoring Jase." He took a breath and shook his head. "I've been thinking about this for a long time."

"Thinking about what? You're not making any sense."

"I had my chance, but you... You haven't Drew. Maybe Sadie and Mae's arrival is a wake-up call. Let someone else manage the ranch. Like me."

"You want me to give up the ranch?"

"No. I'm saying step back some. After nearly twenty years, haven't you earned the right? There's no reason why you have to be available twenty-four seven and have your finger in every pie." Trevor lifted a gloved hand. "Or maybe we should sit down and discuss restructuring the chain of command around here. We've been doing things the same way since I was a kid. Could be time for a change."

Drew sucked in a breath, feeling the punch to his midsection. Trevor was right, they had been doing things the same since their father was alive. Was it time for a change? Or did his brother think he was getting too old to manage the ranch? Either way, Trevor had given him a lot to think about.

"Let me pray on it."

"Fair enough."

"Was there something else? Because now I'm late."

"I'm happy to teach Sadie how to ride." Trevor pushed back the brim of his hat. "Unlike you, I don't have a personal interest in the lady in question."

"Not a chance."

"Yeah, that's what I thought you'd say." He chuckled. "You're awfully protective of the woman. What's going on? Sadie was a burr under your saddle when she arrived."

"I gotta go," Drew growled.

Trevor's eyes rounded, and his jaw slacked as he stared at Drew. "Are you kidding me? You and Sadie?"

"There is no me and Sadie."

"Yeah, right. You're telling the wrong person. You best watch yourself before you find yourself tangled up with a woman who's leaving town."

"Trev, you're overstepping here."

His brother shook his head. "Don't say I didn't warn you."

"It's a riding lesson." Drew turned on his heel and headed for the stables, muttering beneath his breath all the way, and trying to figure out how Trevor had made the ridiculous leap to him being tangled up with Sadie.

He turned the corner into the stable yard and stopped.

"Sadie?"

The woman sat astride Silver outside the stables, holding the reins like an old pro.

He pulled off his hat and then put it back on. "How? When?"

"One of your wranglers. Joe, I think he said his name

is. Joe helped me find Silver and showed me where your tack room is. He got me all fixed up."

"Joe tacked up Silver for you?"

"No." Indignation streaked across her face. "*I* saddled the horse. I just needed to be oriented to your facility."

"I could have done that."

She glanced at her watch. "You're fifteen minutes late. Joe was very helpful, and we chatted. Did you know that he and his wife are adopting twin babies?"

"No. I guess I didn't know that. You covered a lot of ground in fifteen minutes."

"Oh, I was here thirty minutes early. I don't like to be late."

"Like me," Drew muttered. He ran a hand over his face as his conversation with Trevor echoed.

"Are we still going to ride?" she asked.

"Yeah, though it appears to me that you may have misled me on your qualifications."

Sadie shook her head. "No. Not at all."

"Hmm. From where I'm standing, it appears that you led me to believe you were green. Turns out you're a ringer."

She frowned. "No, I'm neither. I told you I wanted to prep for this, so I did."

"And I can see that you are prepped." He assessed her from head to toe. Instead of a cowboy hat, she wisely wore a helmet. Still, she managed to look like a model for the cover of some cowgirl magazine. Plaid Western shirt and denim vest. Check. Wranglers so new the crease could cut butter. Check. Then his gaze landed on her footwear in the stirrups.

They weren't just boots. Floral embroidery detailed the foot and collar. With a square toe and pull tab, the honey-brown leather had to be the softest-looking boots he'd ever seen.

"Those are some boots."

Face alarmed, Sadie looked down at her feet. "What's wrong with my boots?"

"They must have cost a day's paycheck."

"You told me to get a good pair. Tracey at the Hitching Post assured me these are top quality."

"Tracey, huh? Well, Tracey wasn't wrong." He smiled. No use telling her a pair of plain brown ropers would have done the trick. Sadie did like her pretty footwear. "Let me tack up. I'll be with you real quick."

Minutes later, he walked his stallion up to Silver. "Before I have to eat my hat, maybe you ought to tell me about this prep work."

"Six books, dozens of online videos and three hours with Sweet Pea."

He couldn't believe what he was hearing. Bess had conspired behind his back. "You rode Sweet Pea? Are you telling me that Bess gave you a lesson already?"

She sighed. "Apparently, I am, though I wasn't supposed to tell."

"Bess." He laughed. "I should have known."

"I don't think it's funny."

"That's because you didn't just get played." He gave her a critical assessment. "But you're looking good. Excellent posture. You might want to relax those shoulders. There won't be any quizzes today."

Sadie took a deep breath and smiled. "That's good because I'm all studied out."

"Can you handle a short trail ride? Silver knows the trail better than I do. It's a well-worn path through the pasture. No brush or trees to worry about."

"Does that mean I follow you, or you follow me?"

"I think it's best if you follow me. I can check the ground as we go."

"Okay."

"Now, remember, sit right in the middle of the saddle, hands still. Always look in the direction you want to go. More importantly, relax, and take a deep breath. If you're nervous, Silver will feel it." He searched her face. "You feel comfortable about this?"

"I do. Silver's a very chill horse. Is she as old as Sweet Pea?"

Drew laughed. "Mature. We don't want to hurt her feelings."

"Mature."

He cued his horse and took the lead. They rode in silence for a few minutes, with only the plodding movement of the horse's hooves on the trail and the twitter of birds in the trees. A perfect April day in Oklahoma. Not too humid, with enough breeze that the scent of wildflowers in bloom escorted them across the pasture.

"You doing okay back there?" he called.

"Yes."

"See that patch of trees to the right?"

"Uh-huh."

"We're going that way. Just follow me. Slow and easy. We're in no rush."

"I specialize in slow."

Once he approached the cluster of maple trees, Drew eased from his horse and wrapped the reins around a low-hanging branch. He walked over to Sadie and Silver. "Let me help you down."

"I've got it. I practiced my mount and dismount a couple dozen times."

"On a horse?"

Again, her face reflected indignation. "Yes. On a horse."

Drew's lips twitched.

Sadie's dark brows knit together, and her lips thinned. "Are you laughing?"

"No, ma'am. Not me." He stood in front of Silver, hand on the bridle in case Sadie needed assistance or the horse got spooked.

"Really, Drew. I've got this. I'm a greenhorn, but I can dismount."

"Anyone can dismount. The key is to do so without kicking the horse or falling on your backside."

Sadie moved the reins to her left hand and gripped Silver's mane. Then she took her right foot out of the stirrup and over the rear of the horse. Leaning against the horse, hands on the pommel and cantle, she dismounted gently with both feet landing on the ground.

Drew blinked. She'd done it.

"Nice job." He lifted the stirrups and took the reins while she pulled off her helmet and shook her dark hair free.

He couldn't help but stare as the chocolate tresses moved around her head like silk. Sadie reminded him of a butterfly coming out of its cocoon. A pretty butterfly.

She grinned widely and then looked around. "This is a beautiful spot."

"It is, and it's not too far off the beaten trail." He nodded toward the right. "Come on. There's a stream on the other side of those trees."

Sadie followed until they both stood overlooking a stream where clear foams of water rushed over slick and worn moss-covered rocks. Prettiest place on the ranch, in his opinion. Made him smile and thank the good Lord for all His blessings.

"See that grove of trees on the other side of the stream?" He pointed. "That's where I want to build my house."

Sadie's eyes followed his finger. "You're going to build a house?"

"Sure, we're all given a parcel to build on the family spread. Sam has a house not far from here. Built it when he was going to get married. Trevor built a house for his wife years ago. Lucas lives with him these days."

"What's the significance of this spot? I mean, besides being peaceful and beautiful."

"I planted those fruit trees nearly twenty years ago after my folks died. There's apple, peach, cherry and pecan. Reminds me of them. The location? This spot means that I can hear the creek at night and catch a glimpse of the main house at all times."

Sadie turned around. "You can't see the main house from here."

"Ah, but I'll be able to when I'm sitting on the balcony of the second floor, with my boots on the rail, sipping coffee."

"I like that visual. How did you figure that out?"

"Climbed a tree."

"Very clever." She looked in the direction of the Morgan house. "That homestead means a lot to you, doesn't it?"

"Yeah. It does. My mother inherited enough money from her grandmother to buy the land and build the house. She and my father were only twentysomething when they decided to start Lazy M."

"You and your brothers are second-generation ranchers." She nodded. "You're fortunate to have such a legacy of love."

Drew nodded. "You're right. No one's ever said it quite like that. It is a legacy of love." He turned to her. "What about you, Sadie?" he asked carefully. "Do you know anything about your parents?"

"No. I was left at a fire station as a baby." Her face remained impassive as she spoke.

Abandoned as a baby and returned when she got older. Drew sucked in a breath. No wonder Sadie went through life alone. Except for Delia. It was by choice, not chance. Everything made sense now, like her drive for perfection, to do it all right and stay in control. She was the only thing she could trust in her life.

"I'm sorry."

She turned to him. "Please don't pity me."

"I don't pity you. I think you're an amazing person who deserved better."

"I had Delia. She was my better, which is why I'm determined to give Mae better as well."

Drew nodded.

For a minute, they were silent, listening to water pushing its way downstream.

"If you build your own place, then what will your grandfather do in that big house all by himself?" she asked.

"Hmm?" He met her gaze. "The house? Oh, I've been nudging him to invite his widowed sister to come live with us. Aunt Dolly. She's in Texas, though we have never held that against her."

A wisp of a smile touched Sadie's lips. "Dolly?"

"Short for Delores. She stayed with us awhile after the folks died. Sweet as can be, and even Bess likes her. It's getting to be time for Bess to think about retiring. More than time, but she won't retire as long as she's needed."

"Who'll feed the crew if Bess retires?"

"I'll figure that out as I go."

Overhead, a red-tailed hawk circled low in the sky, searching for prey. It released a hoarse cry as it soared past.

Sadie watched its flight, then turned to Drew. "You have big plans."

He shrugged. "Don't you? Surely, an organized gal like yourself has a five-year plan."

"Sure. Tenure. Write a few more articles for publication. Keep teaching. Build my retirement fund. It all seemed so important once." She sighed. "That was before Delia and Jase."

"Yeah, everything changed when we lost them."

"Uh-huh." She kicked at the ground with the toe of her fancy boot and sighed.

"Ever think about staying in Homestead Pass?"

She frowned and cocked her head. "What would I do here?"

"I don't know. Just throwing it out there. Have you considered the possibility of a remote position? Homestead Pass is remote." He smiled, hoping to lighten things up.

"I… I…" She stammered and stared at him, eyes wide. "I hadn't thought about staying."

"Well, maybe you should." The words slipped out before he could think about the wisdom. Then he didn't care. He might be slow to realize it, but now that he'd said the words, he knew they were true.

"Is that a bug?" Sadie swatted at her face and shivered, brushing at her dark hair.

He leaned in, reached for the bit of dried leaf in her hair and froze when he realized how close he was to her lips. Close enough to smell cinnamon. Close enough to consider touching his lips to hers.

"You smell like coffee cake," he said.

Sadie looked up at him, her chocolate eyes clear and trusting. "Do I?" She smiled. "Full disclosure. I have a couple of slices of Bess's coffee cake in my pocket, along with a little survival kit in case something happened."

Drew smiled. "I'd expect nothing less."

Her chin inched up. "I like to be prepared."

"Yep. I get that now."

Heart pounding, hand trembling, he removed the offending leaf and stepped back, far away from the scent of cinnamon and things he couldn't, shouldn't, have. "We should go."

"Did I do something wrong?" Was that disappointment he heard in her voice?

"Wrong? No. You do everything right."

She frowned, clearly confused, as she searched his face.

"Make no mistake. I want to kiss you," he said softly. 'Not because you're beautiful and I'm attracted to you. Those things fade. But because you're smart, compassionate, good and kind." He took a deep breath. "But I won't. It would be wrong for us to cross that line when there are so many decisions to be made."

Wrong, and yet he kicked himself for doing the right thing.

"Thank you," she murmured.

An awkward silence settled between them as they walked to the horses.

"Need help getting on Silver?" he asked.

"Yes, unless you have a mounting block hidden out here."

"I don't." Drew laughed. "If I help you, maybe you'll share that cinnamon cake."

Sadie pulled on her helmet and met his gaze. "I could do that." She grinned, and the tension between them disappeared.

Drew locked his fingers together and gave her a boost with his hands. Then he stepped back as she settled in the saddle and took up the reins.

"You make a fine-looking cowgirl, Sadie Ross."

Mighty fine. As though she belonged here, on that horse, on this ranch, in Homestead Pass. Could he convince Sadie of that? He released a breath. And if so, did he have the courage to overcome the wall of fear he'd built around his heart?

Chapter Seven

Sadie peeked at Drew. Hands on the wheel, he concentrated on the road before them. It had been a three-hour drive from the pediatric cardiologist's office in Tulsa, yet they'd barely spoken a word.

"Almost home," Drew said as the Welcome to Homestead Pass sign came into view.

"Maybe we should talk before we get back to the house," Sadie said.

"Okay. What are you thinking?"

"Mae's surgery has been scheduled. That's all I can think about." She glanced into the back seat at Mae, who was now asleep in her car seat. Blond curls created a halo around the baby's head, and her pink lips formed a bow in slumber. "She looks so perfect. Maybe she's a little small for her age but is that such a big deal?"

"The doctor mentioned an elevated blood pressure. Taking care of the hole in her heart will ensure she doesn't have lung damage as she grows."

Sadie nodded. Yes, she understood the facts, but the facts failed to stop her anxiety. She found herself sighing repeatedly. Drew would say she had her fret-face on. There was no denying it. Yes, she was fretting.

"It's good news that Dr. Bedford wants to do the transcatheter procedure instead of open-heart surgery," he continued. "And she and her staff have lots of experience with the procedure. They're the best in the entire state."

"You're right. I need to focus on the positive. I am grateful for a specialist who is so familiar with the procedure."

Drew hummed in agreement. "And once we get home, Bess will call the church ladies and start a prayer chain."

Sadie had met Bess's friends. The women were powerful prayer warriors. She swallowed, once again working to stay calm. "I want to be like Bess and her friends," she said. "And I'm trying to stand in faith, but fear is trying hard to take over." She looked at him. "You know?"

He reached over and took her hand. "I do. Fear. Anxiety. It's suffocating. Makes it hard to breathe. Hard to think of anything else."

"Yes," Sadie whispered. She looked down at their entwined hands. How was it that her hand in his felt so right?

"I'll tell you what Gramps told me nearly twenty years ago," Drew said. He met her gaze for a moment, his blue eyes comforting. "We're in this together. You aren't alone. And when you need to be lifted up to the Lord, I'll do it, and I'll expect you to do the same."

"Yes, of course." For a moment, Sadie simply rested in the knowledge that she had someone to share the burden. Someone who reminded her to cast her cares upon the Lord. "I appreciate you, Drew."

"Back atcha, Sadie."

For minutes, the only sound was the rhythmic thumping of tires on asphalt.

"Is that your phone?" Drew asked.

"Is it?" Sadie dug in her purse. "Yes. It's the attorney."

"Put it on Speaker."

"Mr. Whitaker, this is Sadie Ross. Drew is driving, so I have you on Speaker."

"Dr. Ross, good afternoon. Where are you and Mr. Morgan on decision-making for the guardianship of Mae Franklin?"

The calm she'd been fighting for inched further away. "Please, can you give us a little more time? Mae is scheduled for a medical procedure."

"I wasn't aware," the lawyer said slowly. "I would be remiss not to share that I have concerns about timing since Helen's health is precarious. I'd like to have all the paperwork completed, along with the background check, to prevent a potentially difficult situation."

"Difficult situation?" Sadie sat straight up in her seat. Alarm bells began to go off in her head.

The attorney seemed to hesitate for a moment. "As I previously advised, if neither of you is willing to assume guardianship, and because there are no other relatives, Mae could be turned over to the Department of Human Services for temporary foster placement."

Sadie's heart began to race. "But one of us *has* agreed to assume guardianship! We just haven't decided which one." She glanced at Drew.

"I encourage you to decide immediately," Whitaker replied, "so we can file the documents and schedule family court."

"Her procedure is in two weeks. We'll reach out as soon as she's discharged."

"I'll make a note of that. In the meantime, I'd like you to visit with someone from Child Support Services at DHS."

"Oh?" Sadie frowned. Why someone from DHS?

"Not in an official capacity," the attorney continued. "Her name is Kimberly Smith. I believe she can assist you with the decision-making process and answer any questions you may have."

"If you think it's necessary," Sadie said.

"I believe it is. Would early this evening be convenient?"

"Today?" Sadie blinked. They'd left for Tulsa at six in the morning and, after four hours of appointments and testing with Mae, were headed home in time for dinner.

She looked at Drew and was surprised at his vigorous nod.

"Yes, sir," he said. "We'll make it work."

When the call ended, he glanced at Sadie. "Did you get what he was trying to say?"

"Apparently not."

"Whitaker wants all the paperwork signed, sealed and delivered in the event that Helen takes a turn for the worse. Can't fault him for that. He's got Mae's best interests in mind."

"What do we do now?" she asked.

"Pray for Helen, for starters."

"Yes. Of course."

"Then we'll listen to what this Kimberly Smith has to say, get through Mae's procedure, and determine what is best for Delia and Jase's baby."

"Two weeks from now." Sadie repeated what the scheduling nurse had said. And then what?

She turned to look out the passenger window as the town passed by. Though her life and career were in Tulsa, each day, she fell more in love with Homestead Pass. And despite herself, she found that she cared for the manager of the Lazy M Ranch far more than she could have predicted. Wasn't it only a couple weeks ago she'd bristled at each conversation?

Mae had taught two opposites to meet in the middle. No matter what was decided, soon, Drew and Homestead

Pass would be only a memory. The thought left her heart aching with loss because the end of this road, this journey, fast approached.

Later, when the dinner dishes were done, and Mae was sleeping, Sadie stared outside the kitchen window, where rain continued to tap against the glass. The house was quiet. Bess had long since gone home and Gramps had retired to his room when he'd heard the social worker was coming.

But where was Drew? How long did it take to gas up his vehicle and 'be right back'?

She wiped the countertops one more time and peeked in on Mae. Then she checked her phone. Nothing.

The kitchen wall clock continued to tick, minute by minute, emphasizing how time kept marching forward despite her concerns.

The sound of the front door opening had her rushing to the hallway. "Drew?"

"Yeah. It's me."

The man was soaking wet. When he moved to slip off his boots, moisture dripped from his hat to the floor.

"What happened to you?" she asked.

Drew shot her a sheepish look. "Now, that's a long story. Why don't I start at the beginning." He pulled off his hat and put it on a wall peg. "I stopped to gas up the dually, and the sky opened up. Out of the corner of my eye, I saw something dash across the road. Turns out, it was the neighbor's dog. Took a good thirty minutes before I could persuade him to get in my truck, so I could drive him home."

"You rescued a dog." Why was she not surprised? Gus was right. Drew had a penchant for rescuing.

"What else could I do?" he asked.

"Maybe you should hurry and go change before our appointment."

He returned shortly after, just as the doorbell buzzed. They both turned toward the sound, then looked at each other and made a nearly comical dash for the door to usher their guest in.

"You can call me Kim," the woman said once seated at the kitchen table. "I work with Child Support Services at the Oklahoma Department of Human Services."

"Thank you for coming by," Sadie said.

"My pleasure." She smiled at Sadie.

"How do you know Mr. Whitaker?" Drew asked.

Kim offered a tender smile. "Mr. and Mrs. Whitaker adopted my younger brother and me after fostering us for a year. That's why I am stressing that this is not an official visit or inspection. I have years of experience, and I've adopted and fostered myself. I'd like to chat and perhaps guide you into thinking deeper about guardianship and possibly adoption." She paused. "However, I'm not here to make decisions for you."

Drew nodded while Sadie clasped her hands tightly in her lap, cutting off the circulation to her fingers.

"So, tell me. How are things going?" Kim asked, her voice gentle.

"Just fine," Drew said. He looked at Sadie as if seeking to corroborate his response.

"Dr. Ross?"

"Good. Things are good." The wall clock mocked her with each *tick, tick, tick.*

"So, everything is wonderful? Unicorns and rainbows?" Kim nodded. "Okay."

Drew shifted uncomfortably but said nothing.

"I see you have a schedule. Mealtimes and appointments.

Very nice." Kim glanced toward the dry-erase board. "I'm so impressed with how well you two work together."

"Yeah, Dr. Ross… Sadie…is very organized. It's made a big difference."

Kim smiled. "How are you balancing your careers and Mae?"

"I'm on leave," Sadie said.

"And I'm…learning how to juggle a baby and the ranch."

"I see." Kim nodded. "And Mae is having a surgical procedure in two weeks."

"Yes," Sadie returned.

"I understand that procedure is the milestone that stands between both of you and a decision about the future. Do you have tentative plans for after the procedure?"

"Plans?" Drew looked at Sadie.

Sadie frowned. "We've spent so much time adjusting to this new normal, learning how to take care of Mae's day-to-day needs and managing our own schedules, that we haven't had time to think about a plan."

Or maybe they were both terrified of a plan. Sadie blinked at the shocking revelation. She'd been all about planning when she arrived, with each step taking her closer to the precipice of the future. Yet, she hadn't allowed herself to think beyond the cardiology appointment and now the procedure.

Could it be that she and Drew were purposely moving the goalpost to avoid making a decision?

"That's okay," Kim said. "Perhaps you can tell me why you want to accept guardianship." She looked to Drew first.

"Jase was my best friend. I want to honor him by raising his child. This ranch, and the close-knit community here in Homestead Pass, is a great place to do that. I have a huge support system in this town."

Sadie tried not to sigh. His platform certainly out-weighed hers.

Kim faced her. "And you, Sadie?"

"I spent most of my life in the foster care system," Sadie said. "Much of it with Mae's mother." She paused, working for the courage to say what was in her heart. "I know that my history makes me uniquely qualified to understand the responsibilities of accepting guardianship and adoption in the future."

Kim offered a thoughtful nod. "You two have stepped up in the middle of a crisis. I think you're amazing. Give yourself some credit. You've been in survival mode, with no real opportunity to consider the long-term. Perfectly understandable. Though I encourage you to remember that guardianship is not about you. It's about Mae. With that in mind, I caution you not to allow guilt to be part of your decision-making process."

"Guilt." Sadie murmured the word. Was that what she was doing?

Kim leaned forward. "I try to get folks thinking about reality instead of romanticizing this huge life choice. Guardianship is forever. That means terrible twos through the terrible teens. Or perhaps it will be smooth sailing. Whatever comes your way. It's yours."

The woman gave them each a slow and pointed look before continuing.

"Parenting means you do everything, fix everything, and no one thanks you. If you are okay with that for about twenty years, then you should proceed."

"That seems pretty cynical," Drew said.

"Does it?" Kim smiled. "I've been in this business a long time, and it's devastating when I see folks go blindly into adoption or guardianship thinking life will be like a television commercial for the perfect, happy family, laughing and smiling to choreographed music. *Perfect* and *family* don't even belong in the same sentence. The satisfaction of parenting comes at unexpected and cherished moments. While there are many blessings, there are also many challenges."

Sadie listened intently. Every word Kim had said so far was absolutely true.

"I would much rather provide prospective parents with raw footage and have them proceed based on facts than be called in the middle of the night with an urgent plea to remove a child because of unrealistic expectations." Kim's gaze reflected anguish, and there appeared to be no triumph in the admission. "Because that happens," she said softly.

Sadie froze at the words. Words she had lived. Clearly, this woman, too, had lived through the devastating pain of rejection.

There was silence for a long moment before Kim began again.

"I'd like you both to consider what accepting guardianship will mean to the other person. Will you be open to visitation? How would that work if one of you or both of you marry?"

Sadie looked at Drew, and his face reflected the same surprise as hers. They hadn't thought that far into the future.

When Kim departed an hour later, Sadie sat at the kitchen table, shell-shocked.

"That was not how I expected the evening to go," Drew said. He slid into a chair across from her.

"I don't know about you," Sadie said. "But I am emotionally exhausted. My brain is mush."

"Yeah. That describes how I'm feeling."

"What do you think about her idea to write down all the

potential pros and cons of guardianship without showing each other the list?"

He released a long breath and ran a slow hand over his face. "I get that it forces us to be honest with ourselves. If you're asking if I'm ready for that kind of honesty, the answer would be no."

Sadie nodded. She felt foolish for all the time spent trying to be the perfect substitute mother for Mae when perfection didn't matter at all. What Mae really needed was someone who was willing to give her love and support for the rest of her life, no matter how messy or imperfect the result. That was the commitment Sadie needed to make.

Drew poked his head into the kitchen and looked around. The room was empty except for Bess at the counter studying a cookbook.

"Psst. Bess," he whispered.

"What are you up to?" She wiped her hands and stepped toward him.

He held out a sheaf of papers. "I was reviewing the terms of Delia and Jase's will."

"Why?"

"That woman from DHS got me a bit rattled. Anyhow, will you look at this?" He pointed to a line on the top document.

"Well, my goodness. It says that Sadie's birthday is today," Bess said.

"Shh. Not so loud. She's changing Mae's diaper."

"Why didn't she tell us it was her birthday?"

"Good morning." Gus gave a nod as he entered the kitchen with the newspaper in his hand. He looked between Bess and Drew. "What are you two whispering about?"

"Shh," Bess said.

"Don't shush me." Gus huffed. "I deserve to know."

"Today is Sadie's birthday, Gramps."

"Why do we have to whisper?" his grandfather asked.

"Because she doesn't know that we know," Drew said.

Gramps shrugged. "Then maybe we should mind our own business."

"Gus," Bess said sternly. "Sit down and have a cinnamon roll."

"Yes, ma'am."

"What should we do?" Bess asked.

"I don't know, but Sadie deserves something nice," Drew replied. "She's done nothing but help everyone else since she arrived in Homestead Pass." As he spoke, the reality of his words hit him. Wasn't it about two weeks ago that Sadie had arrived in town, leaving the comfort of her world and immediately adapting to theirs? She hadn't complained once, though she'd taken on the bulk of the childcare duties.

He was determined that this year, Sadie had a birthday she wouldn't forget.

"What do you think, Bess?" he asked.

The housekeeper tapped her lips with a finger and then grinned, her eyes bright. "You take her and Mae out for a while and a half, and I'll get things rolling."

"I can do that," Drew said.

"What's going on?" Sadie stepped into the kitchen with Mae in her arms. She looked at the wall clock and then the dry-erase board. "I thought this was my day to feed Mae breakfast so Drew could get an early start on chores."

"Chores?" Drew searched for a response. "Oh, yeah, chores. I'm headed to Elk City to pick up a supply order."

Trevor was going to pitch a fit when he found out Drew was missing in action again. Maybe it was time to discuss his brother's ideas for restructuring, because he was right on one count. Things around the Lazy M were changing.

"And he's going to stop at the garden store and pick up seeds for me while he's there," Bess said. "Right, Drew?"

Drew looked around, working to follow the conversation. "Seeds. Yep. I'm picking up seeds."

"What kind of seeds?" Gramps asked. "I was thinking we ought to try watermelon this year."

"We can get watermelon." Drew leaned against the refrigerator, doing his best to appear nonchalant. He glanced at Sadie. "You haven't gotten out much. How about coming with me? I'll spring for lunch for you and Mae."

"Lunch?"

His grandfather laughed and turned the page of his newspaper. "You're going to bruise his ego there, Sadie. Don't you know that most women in this town would jump at an invitation to lunch with Drew?"

"Thanks for the vote of confidence, Gramps. Maybe she doesn't want to get out of the house."

"No. It's not that," Sadie said. "I was trying to remember if I had a meeting this morning."

"You're on leave," Drew said.

"I still like to check in with my teaching assistant weekly. However, it's Friday, so I'm available. Mae and I would love to go to Elk City." That was a relief. Their plan had nearly tanked before it got out of the chute.

"Could you stop at the farmers' market, Drew?" Bess asked. "I'd like that goat cheese from Anderson Farms."

"Sure thing." He looked to his grandfather for assistance with the ruse. "Gramps, you need anything while we're out?"

"Nope."

"You're sure?"

His grandfather looked up from the paper, confusion on his face. "Farmers' market? Well, you might see if they have that fresh kettle corn and maybe some of that home-made jerky."

Drew nodded, making a mental note. "I can do that."

"Now that you mention it, I have been craving pie. Sometimes those church ladies sell rhubarb pie. If there's no rhubarb, get the gooseberry."

"Pie. Okay, that's plenty, Gramps."

"You're the one who asked," his grandfather groused.

Drew turned back to Sadie. "When can you be ready to leave?"

"If you feed Mae breakfast, I'll get ready."

"Fair enough." He took Mae from her and placed her in her high chair.

The minute Sadie left the room, Bess grabbed a pencil and paper and started writing. "Drew, I hope you realize that you're going to have to keep her busy until supper."

"Okay, but Trevor is not going to be happy."

His grandfather gave a hoarse chuckle. "There's an understatement."

Bess pointed her pencil in Gus's direction. "I'm going to need you to run and let the boys know they're expected to be here this evening."

"I don't run." Gramps kept reading the paper.

"I'll invite a few other folks, and we'll have a nice buffet." She scribbled on her pad again.

Gus perked up. "That sounds like a party to me. And where there's a party, there's food."

Bess shot him a pointed look. "If you want to come to the party, you've got to help with the preparations."

Gramps folded up his paper. "I'll get the boys straight off."

"I thought you might."

Drew grabbed a banana from the counter and rice cereal from the cupboard. "Text me if you need anything out in the world, Bess."

"Oh, sure," his grandfather mumbled. "Give her an open invitation and shut me down because I want rhubarb pie."

"I'll get the pie, Gramps." Drew sighed. "Just be sure you help Bess. Remember, we're doing this for Sadie. She doesn't talk about her past much, but I gather that she hasn't had a lot of nice in her life. Today, we're going to change that."

Gus nodded. "I like this plan."

"Me too," Drew agreed. He opened the banana and smiled at his little charge. "You better eat up, Mae-girl. It's going to be a long day."

A long day was an understatement, Drew realized, as he adjusted the baby carrier on his chest. Mae had slept through most of the morning. When they'd completed all of Bess's imaginary errands, Drew added a few more to the list and lingered over a long lunch.

He'd gotten the easy part of this mission. Hanging out with Sadie was more fun than he'd had in a long time. Though, he didn't know how he was going to draw out the afternoon at the farmers' market. There were only so many vendor booths.

"Do you want me to carry her for a while?" Sadie asked. "You've had her since lunch, and it's nearly three."

"I'm good."

"Is my nose red?" Sadie touched her nose gingerly.

"A bit pink." He smiled. She was cute with her pink nose and gaudy sunglasses on the top of her head.

Sadie pulled sunscreen from her purse and swiped more on her face. "I'm glad we put sunscreen and a bonnet on Mae, but I guess I should have worn a hat too."

"That's why God made cowboy hats." He tapped his own.

She laughed. "God didn't make straw Stetsons. And I'd feel like a rhinestone cowboy if I wore a hat like that."

"Do I look like a rhinestone cowboy?"

"No, but you're the real deal. I'm a college professor."

"You ride horses and live on a ranch," he countered. "You're the real deal too, Sadie."

"Temporarily."

He didn't have a response. Didn't want to think about the decisions they had to make and a future without Sadie, maybe even without Mae. Nope, not today.

"Oh, look at that." Sadie darted in front of him to a booth where the vendor displayed skinny hammered sterling silver bangles. "How pretty."

"Get yourself one."

"No. I don't wear much jewelry."

"It's not much jewelry. It's one very sophisticated silver band."

"Maybe another time." She moved on to the next vendor, and he trailed behind, puzzled. If she liked the bracelet, why didn't she buy one? Seemed simple enough.

"Sir, your wife dropped these."

"My wife." He looked at the bright red sunglasses the woman held. "Thank you." It didn't escape his notice that this was the second time someone had referred to Sadie as his wife, and he hadn't bothered to correct either of them.

Could he see himself married? Married to someone like Sadie?

For a lifetime?

For the first time, a calm filled him at the thought, instead of panic. He wasn't sure what to think, because Sadie was leaving, and there wasn't a future to consider, much less a lifetime.

He picked up his pace, caught up with Sadie and put the glasses in her hand.

"Thank you," she said.

"Come on. Let's put a dent in my list," he said.

An hour later, they sat on a bench eating ice cream.

"I hope we're done," Sadie said. "Because I'm exhausted."

He pointed to her blouse, where a blob of chocolate landed.

"Great." She dabbed at the spot with her napkin.

Drew checked his watch. "I, uh… I need to get Gramps's kettle corn."

"Kettle corn. Right. Well, I'm going to go to the restroom while you do that. Let me take Mae and check her diaper. We'll meet you over there by that flower vendor."

When she left, he turned around and started back down the row of vendors they had just passed. By the time he'd finished his business and grabbed the kettle corn, he found Sadie and Mae in the flower stall, admiring a bouquet of tulips.

She eyed him. "Long line for kettle corn?"

"Yep." He nodded to the flowers in front of her. "Which is your favorite?"

"Peonies." She pointed to a bucket filled with pink blossoms on long green stalks.

"No hesitation there. Why peonies?"

"Besides being lovely and fragrant and the fact that the cut flowers last a long time?"

"Yeah, besides that."

"They're a symbol of good fortune. That's why they're included in bridal bouquets."

"You're taking a practical approach."

Sadie laughed. "Yes. That's me. Always practical."

"I can help you with that problem." With the flick of his wrist, Drew caught the eye of the vendor and pointed to the peonies.

"What problem? What are you doing?" Sadie asked.

"Buying flowers."

"Drew, I can buy my own flowers."

"Yep, you can." He leaned close. "But here's a secret. You don't always need to." The vendor wrapped the flowers in green floral waxed paper and handed them to him, and he turned to Sadie. "Would you hold these while I grab my wallet?"

"Drew."

"Sadie."

"Fine." She held the giant bouquet close and inhaled. "Thank you for the flowers. They're beautiful."

He allowed himself to admire the pale pink cabbage-like blossoms and the woman for a moment. "Yep, beautiful."

"Can we go home now?"

"I, um…" How was he going to stall until Bess gave him the okay? "You know, I'd like to grab a bag of those cinnamon pecans before we head out."

She looked at him, eyes rounded. "Seriously? The ones that were at that booth where you just bought Gus's kettle corn? The booth that is nearly at the other end of this row?"

"Yeah, that one."

"Okay, I'll run ahead and pay for them and meet you there."

"What's the rush?"

"We've been wandering around Elk City for days," she said.

He laughed. "Hours. Not days."

"Tell my feet that." She started moving ahead of him.

Drew's phone buzzed, and he glanced at the screen. Bess.

Everything is ready.

He typed k and hit Send before sliding the phone back into his pocket.

"Sadie," he called out. "Wait up."

She turned. "What is it?"

"You're right. Let's forget the pecans. I'm ready to go home."

"What?" She perked up at the words.

"I don't know what I was thinking. My eyes are bigger than my stomach." He held up the shopping bag in his hand. "We've got plenty."

Once they found the truck, Sadie released a heartfelt sigh. She shook her head and buckled her seatbelt. "Next time I go on an excursion with you, remind me to bring roller skates."

"Next time?" Drew grinned. "I like the sound of that." Today was fun, and he couldn't think of anyone else he'd rather spend the day with.

The minute they passed beneath the wooden entrance sign of the Lazy M, Sadie sat up in her seat. "Why are there so many cars in front of the house?"

"Hmm?" He counted six pickup trucks. Now he just needed a good answer.

"Didn't Gramps say his pinochle group was meeting here?"

"Your grandfather plays pinochle?"

"I think so."

"What do you mean? You think so."

"Aw, look. Cooper's waiting for you on the front porch."

"Oh, he is." The dog sat up and barked enthusiastically at their approach. "I'm becoming very attached to that dog," she said.

Relieved at the distraction, Drew pulled into an empty spot, unbuckled his seat belt and jumped out of the truck. "I'll grab Mae. We can get the supplies later."

"Sounds good to me." She reached for Mae's bag.

"I'll get the diaper bag. Maybe you could hold open the front door." He prayed Bess was ready for them.

"I can do that," she said.

Drew picked up a sleeping Mae and began to follow Sadie up the stairs. He paused and held back. "You go ahead. I'm going to grab that kettle corn for Gramps."

The screen door squeaked on its hinges, and a moment later, a chorus of "Happy birthday, Sadie" rang out.

He couldn't help but grin as he pictured Sadie's surprise. "Come on, baby girl," he told Mae. "We have a birthday party to attend."

When he stepped into the house, Sadie had already been swooped up in birthday greetings and conversation. His brothers were in attendance, as well as Chef Moretti, Mrs. Pickett from the bookstore and a few others.

Drew changed Mae's diaper and gave her to Gramps.

"Nice job," his grandfather said as he took the baby. "I didn't think you could do it, but it turns out you've got a bit of sneaky in you, after all. Must be from your grandmother."

"Thanks, Gramps."

"Did you get my pie?"

Drew avoided a response and instead circulated around the room. When Sadie excused herself from a chat with Pastor McGuinness and his wife and slipped into the kitchen, he followed.

"Happy birthday, Sadie," he said. "I'd sing, but I can't carry a tune."

"Thank you." She offered an embarrassed smile while dabbing at the moisture pooled in the corners of her eyes.

"Are you crying?" He rushed to her side. Sure enough, tears threatened to fall.

"Don't be silly. I don't cry. It must be allergies. Oklahoma ranks eighteenth for spring tree pollen, you know."

"Why am I not surprised you know that?" He chuckled.

She swiped at her face and shot him a stern look. "I wish you would have told me about this. I'd have dressed appropriately and maybe avoided spilling chocolate ice cream on myself."

"It wouldn't be a surprise if I told you." He glanced at the dark slacks, floral blouse and fashionable sneakers. "For the record, you look lovely as always."

Sadie gave a slow shake of her head. "Flattery will not get you out of trouble. I cannot believe how sneaky you are."

"You're the second person to say that." Drew grinned. "Let's give credit where credit is due. Bess, Gramps and I are all sneaky and proud of it." He paused. "Were you surprised?"

"Surprised? I was terrified. People were screaming at me."

"It's a surprise birthday party. They're supposed to scream."

"I've never had a surprise birthday party before." She looked at him and then away.

"Now you have," he said softly. He nodded toward the back door. "Come on outside. I want to give you your birthday present."

"You got me a birthday present?"

"Of course. That's what you do on birthdays. Stick with me, and I'll show you how it's done." He held the door to the back porch for her and followed her into the warm evening. Honeysuckle had begun to wrap itself around the porch rail, and its scent drifted to them.

"Here you go." He pulled a small velvet bag from his

pocket and handed it to her. "Usually, birthday presents are wrapped. I didn't have time for that."

She gasped when she pulled the bracelet from the farmers' market bag. "You…you bought the bracelet."

"I get the feeling you have a hard time spoiling yourself."

"Except for shoes," she admitted with an unsteady laugh.

"Yeah, except for shoes." He smiled. "Happy birthday, Sadie," he said again. "I'm glad you could spend it with us."

"Thank you," she breathed. "This is so lovely." She ran a finger over the bracelet's fine inlay. "It's been a really nice day."

"I'm glad." He leaned forward and pressed a kiss to her forehead. "I hope you have many more nice days."

Her eyes met his, and as his heart hammered in his chest, Drew realized it might just be too late to remember Trevor's caution. He was already tangled up with Sadie Ross.

Chapter Eight

Sadie parked her car outside her apartment building and stared at the gray clapboard structure that looked exactly like the other twenty buildings in the complex. She'd never realized before today how depressing the sight was, with the minuscule plots of grass and decorative gravel at each entrance.

The community building divided the east complexes from the west ones. Redbud trees had been strategically planted, along with bright flowers to attract new tenants. Nice, if you liked that sort of obviously landscaped perfection. She preferred the wildflowers that grew in the pasture.

The facility boasted a gym with the latest equipment. Sadie was reminded that on the Lazy M Ranch, six-pack abs came from lifting hay and mending fences, not from a workout room. The space also had an entertainment area with a bar and big-screen television. Her neighbor Amber, a shy divorcée, had told her once that it was where hip singles could mingle during one of the monthly mixers. She'd invited Sadie to come with her.

Not a chance. She might be single, but she was not hip.

Nor did she have plans to ever become hip. Staid and boring was safe.

Behind the community building, there was a small playground. Emphasis on *small*. Sadie cringed at the thought of playing with Mae on that playground. The Greenleaf Apartments were not the wide-open spaces of the Lazy M Ranch.

Sadie checked her watch, gathered the pile of held mail that she'd collected up from the post office, and then walked the short flight of steps to her apartment. She had enough time to check on her place and pick up some clothes before heading to the college for more meetings. As she put her key in the lock, her neighbor stepped into the walkway.

"Sadie. Where have you been? I've missed seeing you in the mornings."

"Hi, Amber," she greeted. "Long story, but I'm taking care of some personal business."

"Personal business… You look fabulous. You have a tan, and your skin is glowing. I've never seen you look so good. You've been working out too, haven't you?"

"I guess I have." Lifting a six-month-old up and down could be considered a free weight. Sadie stifled a giggle.

Amber checked her phone and smiled. "I'm late for an appointment. Call me, and we'll catch up."

"Sure," Sadie said, though she doubted if she would. They'd never had much in common, and now? Well, it occurred to her that she was in limbo right now, living in two worlds. Her academic world and life on the Lazy M Ranch. Suddenly, returning to her world wasn't as enticing as it had been that first day in Homestead Pass.

She opened the door of her apartment and stepped inside. It was a cozy unit with a few fine pieces of furniture that she'd saved to purchase.

Identical to every other one-bedroom apartment in the complex, it was small on space but adequate for her needs—those needs being a comfortable couch for reading and a large desk for work. Because that was basically her life. She put her keys on the small island that separated the living room from the kitchen, next to a large stack of books, and opened the refrigerator.

Two bottles of sparkling water and a yogurt greeted her. She grabbed the water and poured a glass. Glancing around, she sighed. There wasn't even a plant in the place, because she didn't have time to keep a plant alive.

More irony. She was now charged with keeping a baby alive and healthy and happy.

She tried to imagine herself living here with Mae. The idea horrified her. Drew was right. Mae deserved what the Lazy M could offer her.

But how could she walk away from Delia's child when not once had Delia ever walked away from her? The mental battle for what was right for Mae had continued, often keeping her awake at night. She'd begun her list of the pros and cons of guardianship.

Pro: She'd be able to keep Delia's daughter safe and happy.

She owed her friend that much.

Pro: Tulsa had rich cultural opportunities.

But was a six-month-old interested in the Philbrook Museum of Art or the planetarium?

Con: She'd need childcare.

Childcare was expensive, and it meant someone else taking care of Mae. Or maybe she'd look into remote work, as Drew had suggested.

Sadie glanced around. Her apartment, which had suited her for five years, was now wholly unsatisfactory. Another con.

If only she could afford a house with a yard. Maybe it was time to cash in her 401(k).

Sadie opened the French doors and stepped out onto the small balcony. From the back porch of Drew's house, she could see forever. All she could spy from here was the Sushi Bar and Grill across the street. A car horn blared, and she went back inside.

Her cell phone began to ring, and she fished it from her purse. *Drew.*

"Sadie. I hope I'm not interrupting anything."

"No. I'm between meetings." *And it's really good to hear your voice.*

"Everything go as planned?"

"So far. Though the pressure is on to commit to fall semester."

"You haven't decided?"

"How can I, until you and I finalize the plans for Mae?"

"Seems to me, either way, you're going back to Tulsa, right?"

She bristled at his words. Nothing had been decided.

"You never know," she finally said.

"That's pretty much the story of my life. I don't know a thing."

"Was there something you needed, Drew?"

"Yeah, sure. I totally got off topic, didn't I? I called about Mae."

Sadie gripped the cell. "Is she okay? Did something happen?"

"Relax, it's not an emergency. Mae's got a red bottom, and I seem to recall you know how to handle that."

She tried not to laugh. "You know that Bess can handle diaper rash, right?"

"Bess has gone to get the mail, and Mae is unhappy."

"There's a white tube of cream in the changing station.

Second drawer down, next to the wipes. But you might want to let her go without a diaper for a few hours."

"Without a diaper? Are you serious?"

This time Sadie did laugh. "Just put a few towels in the play yard. She'll be fine. Trust me, it works."

"If you say so. You're the expert."

The expert? A couple weeks ago, she hadn't ever held a baby.

"All right, then, thanks for the advice, Sadie. I'll let you get back to whatever it is you're doing."

Doing? She wasn't doing anything important here in Tulsa. Suddenly, nothing seemed as important as what she was doing in Homestead Pass.

"You can call me if you have any other questions."

"Good to know. Be careful driving home."

"I will."

Home. Sadie mulled the word as she played with the silver bracelet on her wrist.

She was standing in her home, wasn't she? Then why didn't it feel like home? She went to her closet and began to pack. One more meeting. Then, maybe if she hurried, she'd get back to Homestead Pass in time for dinner.

Drew peeled off the disposable veterinary gloves and pulled out his buzzing cell phone. The phone had already vibrated a few more times while Drew had been in the process of checking a heifer. It was his brother. "You got an emergency, Sam?"

"Gramps said you were coming to the house in fifteen minutes. It's been an hour."

"Is Mae okay?"

"She might need a diaper change."

"That's why you called me three times?"

"Yeah. What of it?"

"Oh, good night." Drew blew out a breath. "Supplies are in the nursery. Gramps knows where they are. Mind telling me what you're doing at the house?"

"Thought I'd check and see if Bess had any leftover chocolate cake. Gramps had to leave for a doctor's appointment, so I offered to help out. I am her uncle, you know."

"I appreciate that you're helping out." He chuckled at the claim of uncle. "You do realize that makes you *Uncle Sam*, right?"

"You're real funny. I can live with the moniker. Just tell me you're on your way."

"I've just finished evaluating a heifer. Thought it might be a breach, but everything appears normal. I'll be right there."

"I hope so, *Dad.* Because uncles don't do diaper changes."

"Someone's been feeding you disinformation," Drew returned. "And I can guess who." He slipped his phone into a pocket and turned on the water in the barn's basin sink, shaking his head. Lately, he didn't know if he was coming or going. The last week in particular had made him aware of how difficult juggling ranch chores and a baby really was.

"Everything okay?" Lucas asked from behind him.

"Yep. I'm needed at the house. Sadie is in Tulsa for the day."

"What do you want me to do about this little momma?" His brother ran a gentle hand over the flank of the pregnant heifer.

"Keep an eye on her. If she doesn't deliver soon, you'll need to assist."

"You got it."

Drew dried his hands and strode out of the barn, toward the house, with Cooper at his heels. He took the steps two at a time and stopped. "Cooper. Stay. Gramps will have a fit if you come in the house again."

The dog offered a long and martyred whine but complied.

After kicking the dirt off his boots, Drew headed inside.

"That you, Dad?" Sam called. "Hurry on in here. Your daughter is ready for you."

Daughter. He was only recently coming to terms with the phrase *guardian*. Daughter seemed a surreal concept.

Rounding the corner, Drew entered the kitchen. One sniff had him grimacing. "You're sure you don't want the honors?"

Sam offered an adamant shake of his head. "I have things to do."

"I'll take your dish duty tonight if you change Mae's diaper."

Sam narrowed his gaze. Then his eyes lit up, and he grinned. "Gas up my truck too, and we have a deal."

"Okay, fine." Drew sighed and shook his head, feeling guilty for the deal he cut, though he knew that he needed a breather before transitioning to caretaker.

Sam plucked Mae from her high chair. "Come on, little girl, we've got business to attend to."

Drew poured himself a cup of coffee and sank into a kitchen chair just as his grandfather walked in.

"I thought you had a doctor's appointment, Gramps."

"No. I told your brother I had to call and make a doctor's appointment."

"So, where've you been?"

"I, um…" His grandfather frowned as he seemed to search for a response. "Never mind me. Where have *you* been?"

"I run the Lazy M, in case you hadn't noticed."

"Well, yeah, of course. And I was taking care of ranch business as well."

"Was that before or after you realized Mae needed a diaper change?"

"I'm gonna have to plead the Fifth on that one."

"I thought so," Drew muttered. He was quickly learning that everyone wanted to hang out with the adorable, smiling baby, but when she started fussing or needed a diaper change, they scattered like cockroaches when you turned the lights on.

"How'd it go with Sadie shadowing you last week? I never asked."

"Great. She's a hard worker. Eager and enthusiastic. More than I can say for some of the hands I've hired over the years."

"That so?" His grandfather leaned against the refrigerator and eyed Drew thoughtfully.

"What?"

"You might try being sweet to Sadie. Maybe she'll stay in Homestead Pass if you do."

"Sadie is here for Mae. Whatever decision we make, she'll be returning to her life in Tulsa soon."

"You never know. People change." Gramps straddled a kitchen chair backward and folded his arms across the top.

"What are you getting at, Gramps?"

"Nothing. Just chatting with my oldest grandson. You sure are suspicious."

Drew opened his mouth and then closed it, unwilling to give fuel to whatever strategy was fomenting in the wily rancher's mind.

"Remind me why it is you haven't settled down yet?" his grandfather asked.

And there it was, the question Gramps had been dancing around. Drew shook his head and prayed for patience before answering.

"Are you going to psychoanalyze me again, Gramps?"

"Could be."

"Look, besides the fact that I'm not interested in marriage, stop and think about the fact that it's like a frat house around here with four Morgan bachelors and their grandfather in and out. What women would be interested in that? Or the long hours on the ranch. It's been my experience that most women want a whole lot more than I can offer."

"You don't have any experience. I think that's my point here, son."

"True. But why all the interest in my love life lately? I don't poke into yours."

A belly laugh had his grandfather nearly choking with laughter. "Pshaw. I'm widowed. Your grandmother was the love of my life."

Love of his life. Drew smiled at the words. Right now, Cooper was as close as he was going to get to that.

"What are you boys doing in the kitchen?"

Drew turned as Bess stepped into the room with a wicker basket overflowing with clean towels and placed it on the table.

"Man-talk," Gramps said.

Bess chuckled. "Is that right? And where is Mae?"

"Sam is changing Mae's diaper," Drew said.

"No, seriously." Bess chuckled.

"I am serious."

"Well, isn't that an interesting turn of events?" The housekeeper's face said she still wasn't quite certain they were telling the truth.

"Where did you say Sadie went today?" Gramps asked.

"T-Town. She had to take care of business, meet with

her boss and pick up some clothes." Drew glanced at his watch. "Should be back this evening."

"You remember that I'm leaving early today, Drew?" Bess asked.

"Are you threatening me?"

Bess started laughing. "Maybe so. There's a roast in the oven. Someone better take it out when the timer goes off, or you'll be eating cereal for dinner."

"So, I'm taking care of the baby and dinner?"

"You're her guardian," Bess replied.

"Yeah, it seems everyone keeps reminding me of that."

Bess nudged the basket toward Gus. "I could use some help with these towels."

Gramps shook his head and stood. "I would help, but I promised Lucas I'd help him put out hay." He backed out of the room quickly, his boots echoing down the hall.

"That was six hours ago," Drew called with a laugh.

"Never saw a man more allergic to chores," Bess mumbled. She reached for a towel and began to fold, as did Drew.

Minutes later, the sound of the front door opening could be heard. Cooper bounded into the kitchen with Sadie trailing behind. She wheeled a large suitcase in one hand and a briefcase and tote in the other. Half a dozen stacked books wobbled on top of the suitcase.

In a red print dress and heels, Sadie looked very un-Sadie-like. A smile touched her lips when her gaze met his.

"You're looking mighty pretty, Sadie," Bess observed.

Drew concurred and found himself tongue-tied as he took in the professor. Her hair, usually tied back or in a braid, tumbled free around her shoulders, which only abetted his confusion. Where was the Sadie he'd come to know the last few weeks? This woman was a version he had difficulty reconciling to the reticent and tightly wound academic. He found himself both attracted and terrified at the same time.

"Oh, thanks. I had lunch with my department head at some fancy restaurant." She placed the tote on the ground and reached for the stack of books.

"Here, let me help." Drew stood and scooped up the books, placing them on the counter. When he got closer to Sadie, the scent of vanilla wrapped around him, and he stepped back, alarmed. She was wearing perfume.

"Thank you," Sadie said.

"We didn't expect you back so soon," Bess commented.

"I finished earlier than I expected." Sadie smiled at the housekeeper. "And I missed Mae."

"Those books hitched a ride with you?" Drew asked.

She laughed softly as though embarrassed, and he found himself staring. Had he ever heard Sadie laugh before? The sound was as intoxicating as the perfume.

"Pretty much," she said. "I stopped at the big bookstore while I was in Tulsa and picked up a few more baby books."

Drew ducked his head and worked hard not to comment. No use spoiling the moment by pointing out yet again that you didn't learn about life from books.

"I called Helen too," Sadie said.

"How's she doing?" Drew asked.

"She was resting, but I spoke to her friend, who said she had handled her first round of chemo fairly well. Helen is going to stay in Tulsa for now. I got the address, and I'll take some pictures of Mae and send them along."

"That's a wonderful idea," Bess said. She picked up the stack of folded towels. "I'm going to head home. Dinner is in the oven."

"Bye, Bess."

The housekeeper left, and the sound of the clock ticking filled the awkward silence.

"I brought you something," Sadie finally said. She peered at him shyly and then quickly looked away.

"Me?" Drew glanced around.

"Yes." She pulled a baby-blue-and-white-striped box out of the tote bag and handed it to him. "When we were fixing fences, you mentioned those tasty Eagle donuts you bought when you were visiting Rebel, Oklahoma, on a business trip. They have a shop in Tulsa now. I stopped in and got a dozen."

Drew blinked, surprised that she'd remembered the passing comment. "You didn't have to do that."

"It's a little thank-you for welcoming me into your home." She eyed the empty high chair. "Is Mae sleeping?"

Drew placed the box on the table and peeked inside. A dozen perfect maple bars. He couldn't remember the last time someone had done something so thoughtful, and he found himself touched by the gesture.

"Drew, where's Mae?" Sadie repeated.

"Sam is changing her diaper."

"Sam?"

"Yeah, why does everyone find that so surprising?"

"Both your brothers and your grandfather have demonstrated a marked aversion to changing diapers."

"Well, they better get over it. If Mae ends up living on the ranch, they'll be changing diapers regularly. And I'm not filling up their gas tank every time."

"Wait. Wait. Wait." Sadie held up a hand. "Can we back up a minute? You bribed your brother to get him to change a diaper?"

"In my defense, I've been running between the house and the barn all day. I was trying to buy a few minutes of downtime."

"I hate to point out the obvious, but if Mae does end up living on the ranch, as you stated, this is what your life will be every day."

"Not if I hire a nanny, it won't."

Sadie leaned against the kitchen counter and crossed her arms. "A nanny isn't the solution."

Whoa, now he'd done it. Sadie had gone from soft and shy to irked and formidable in less than a minute. Her cheeks were red with emotion, and her expression had morphed into something he'd never seen before. Anger.

"You're mad at me?" he asked.

"I'm mad at the situation. That baby deserves to be raised by her parents. Delia and Jase should be here."

Ah, there it was. Her outburst wasn't about Sam changing a diaper for him. It was about losing their friends.

"We can't keep rehashing the same thing, Sadie. The situation is what it is. We have to move forward."

"I'm not rehashing. This…" She waved a hand around. "This is simply discussing."

"Is that what you call it? Maybe we should discuss the fact that you'll have to have help with Mae if she lives in Tulsa."

"Yes. I've given that some thought while I was in Tulsa. Perhaps I can find a position that's wholly remote."

He blinked, surprised at the response. "You're thinking about that?" The idea put a new spin on their situation because there was no way he could offer to do the same.

"Maybe. I love my career, but I'm starting to consider that there might be other opportunities out there. Is Shakespeare my calling? Or is raising an orphaned baby? Has my life been leading up to this moment? This decision? I don't know, but I'm beginning to think hard about the future."

"Yeah, you sure have been thinking hard."

"Someone has to."

"Ouch," Drew murmured.

"Being in Tulsa, seeing my real life, was a reality check."

"How's that?"

"I realized that Delia had everything I longed for but was afraid to admit. A loving partner, a baby, a home. I love my job. I don't need anything else to complete my life. But there is nothing wrong with admitting I want more."

"Ohh-kay." Drew found himself baffled by her admission. "What's your plan?"

"I plan to challenge you every step of the way for guardianship. You're in this out of the kindness of your heart. Doing the right thing for a friend. I'm here because I want it, with all my heart."

"If you're looking at remote opportunities, then you're not tied to Tulsa."

"I haven't gotten that far."

When the stove beeped, interrupting their discussion, Sadie grabbed oven mitts and pulled open the oven. She stuck a thermometer in the roast and nodded. "It's ready. Maybe you want to call your brothers and get them to clean up while I pull the potatoes out of the Crock-Pot."

"You want help setting the table?" he asked, hesitant to annoy her again.

"I've got it."

She sure did. He stood in awe as Sadie hustled around the kitchen like she'd prepared to serve dinner to five cowboys a million times before.

"Well, look who's home." Sam carried Mae into the kitchen. The baby kicked her legs with delight and reached for Sadie.

"How's my big girl?" Sadie asked. She took Mae into her arms and held her like she was her own. The awkwardness and hesitation of weeks ago had disappeared.

Sadie was a confident caregiver, with plenty of love for her friend's daughter.

The scene before him had Drew's heart aching. Sadie and Mae had only been part of the Morgan household a short time, yet it was as though they'd always been here. Sadie was the natural choice for guardianship.

The irony of the fact that only minutes before, he'd reminded Gramps that Sadie would be gone soon slapped him in the face. How had it happened that he'd gotten used to having Sadie and Mae in his life?

If Sadie had her way, she and Mae would be in Tulsa soon. No, he surely was not ready for that to happen.

Was there a way to keep both Mae and Sadie on the Lazy M? That would require divine intervention. He'd better start praying immediately.

Chapter Nine

Sadie adjusted her laptop and quickly reviewed her calendar while she waited for Leah to join the online meeting. The day's agenda showed this morning's meeting and another cooking class. Gramps had volunteered to babysit if Drew was still working.

Her supervisor appeared on the screen. "Good morning, Sadie."

"Morning, Leah."

"It was lovely to visit with you last week."

"You as well."

"You should know that the dean pulled me aside at Monday's staff meeting. He's impatient for your decision about fall."

Sadie grimaced. "What does that mean?"

"Is the dean aware that even though I'm on family leave, I've still been doing final grading and examination prep? Doesn't that give me some sort of standing?" The words came out in a huff of frustration.

"As an overachiever?" Leah chuckled. "Absolutely. I love you, and so does your teaching assistant. The issue is that the fall academic calendar is already up, and the course schedule is close to finalization." She put on her glasses. "The dean's tunnel vision prevents him from seeing anything but the bottom line. Frankly, I don't know how much longer I can put him off."

Sadie flipped the pages of her planner, processing the upcoming dates. "Doesn't family leave require the college to hold my position?"

"An excellent question. I wondered the same thing and went to Human Resources to verify the information." Leah nodded and shuffled through papers. "Ah, here it is." She paused and lowered her glasses, looking at Sadie with concern. "Remember, I'm on your team, so don't shoot the messenger. HR says that is not how the policy works. The law says 'same or equivalent job.'"

Same or equivalent job. That could put her in the Arts Department teaching basket weaving. She swallowed. Surely not. "That's not good. Not good at all."

"You still have a little wiggle room. You're officially on leave, and I can pretend I haven't been able to reach you. But the clock is ticking. *Loudly.* The sooner you can let me know, the sooner I can call off the dogs." She laughed. "I'm just full of clichés today."

"Leah, I appreciate you."

"I'm glad, because I appreciate you as well. You're a huge asset to our department. Which means you make me look good."

Leah leaned closer to the computer screen. "There is some good news in all this. I'm not supposed to tell you, but has that ever stopped me?"

"What is it?"

She smiled. "Don't you want to guess?"

"The request to paint my office was approved?" Sadie frowned. She hated guessing.

"Think bigger."

"Leah. I'm not a dreamer. You know that."

"Okay, fine. You squeezed it out of me." Leah grinned. "You've been short-listed for the Manchester Award." Leah's smile grew even wider, and she did a little chair dance as she made the quiet announcement.

Sadie's quick intake of air was audible. There was a roaring in her ears as she processed Leah's words. She put a hand to her beating heart.

The Manchester Award? She'd dreamed of this award since she'd started as a teaching assistant.

"Oh, Leah."

"Right? Can you believe it?"

"I thought the Manchester was only for tenured staff," Sadie said.

"Not at all. It's for exceptional staff, and that's you. Besides, you're up for tenure next year, and you're a shoo-in."

"Do you happen to know who nominated me?"

"Me, for one. Think how great that would look on your CV. And the award would provide you a year to study and teach in England."

There was silence between them. Then Leah frowned. "Well, say something."

Sadie didn't know what to say. The nomination was an affirmation of years of hard work and focus. Yet, everything had changed since Delia's death. She was no longer certain if her career was enough.

"Sadie," Leah groaned. "Please, do not tell me you're having second thoughts about coming back to Tulsa."

"I'm having second thoughts about everything."

"You're thirty-six. Few women attain full professor and tenure so young."

"Yes, I'm grateful." Grateful and painfully aware. The clock was ticking everywhere.

"Would you give up the opportunity to teach in London for a ranch in Oklahoma?"

"The deer and the antelope or The Globe Theatre." Sadie laughed. "I've dreamed of attending a play at Shakespeare's own theater."

"And I've always dreamed of fish and chips and a Bakewell tart," Leah added.

Sadie laughed. "That too. Did you know London has three hundred museums?"

"Why am I not surprised that you know that?"

"That's my specialty. Useless trivia." What a sad claim to fame.

"On a serious note, when is Mae's procedure?"

Sadie took a deep breath at the sobering change of topic. "It's coming right up in a week. She'll stay overnight. Maybe you and I can chat, even if it's only in the hospital cafeteria." Sadie paused. "You can meet Drew."

"Yes, your cowboy." The other woman feigned a dramatic swoon.

"He's not *my* cowboy."

"If you say so. And does he have any older brothers?"

"No, but his grandfather is single."

"I won't rule out a handsome cowboy grandfather." Leah studied her computer screen. "Okay, I have the date on my calendar. I'll do my best to dodge questions until after your baby's surgery. But I can only do so much, even for my favorite professor."

"Oh, Leah, thank you. I do understand."

"Now, remember, the official award nominations will be announced at the faculty meeting next Monday. Act surprised when the dean calls."

"Oh, you can be sure that I will still be surprised on Monday."

The Manchester Award. Sadie's thoughts continued to reel after she disconnected from the meeting app.

Her gaze spanned the room, landing on the bouquet of

peonies. Had it really been a week since she'd spent the day with Drew? It had been one of the best days of her life.

A pink petal dropped from the peony, followed by another, landing on the oak bookshelf. The bouquet was fading. Soon it would be only a cherished memory, like her time in Homestead Pass and on the Lazy M Ranch.

Was that what she wanted? There were so many decisions to be made. So many paths. Only prayer could clear the fog and help her see which path led to her future.

A quick rap at the open door had her turning. Drew peeked his head in with Mae. Her heart melted at the sight of the baby in the cowboy's muscled arms.

"Are we interrupting?"

"No. Come in. I thought Bess was with Mae."

"I was passing through, and Bess needed to head into town for groceries. It's only been about fifteen minutes."

"Well, I appreciate it. Thank you."

"Clean diaper on board," he said.

"Thank you for that as well."

He moved closer, and Mae eagerly stretched her arms out to Sadie while babbling 'ah' and 'oh.' When Drew's fingers touched Sadie's as he transferred the child, their eyes connected. He smiled slowly and tenderly, and her traitorous heart sighed in response.

"Got her?" he asked when Mae wrapped her arms around Sadie's neck and cooed with happiness.

"Yes. I have her." Sadie closed her eyes for a moment to savor the sweet baby scent. Never would she take moments like this for granted. Nor would she forget them a week from now, a month from now or a year from now. She knew only too well how quickly circumstances could change.

"Everything okay with your boss?" Drew asked. "You seemed deep in thought when I knocked."

"Did I?" She shrugged. "I mentioned that I'm being

pressured to make a decision about the fall. I may be out of a job if I don't offer an answer soon."

"That's too bad. But making a decision does seem to be the theme around here, doesn't it?"

She nodded. "Have you started on your pro/con list yet?"

Drew cringed. "I've started, but I haven't gotten too far. Between vaccinations, branding and moving the cattle, I've hardly had time to breathe."

"Maybe that's part of the purpose of the exercise."

He pushed back the brim of his hat. "What do you mean?"

She looked at him. "Kim didn't ask us to list our qualifications. She asked us to write down the pros and cons of guardianship."

"I don't follow."

"You and I are like peanut butter and jelly."

"Peanut butter and jelly." He nodded. "I can live with that."

"No, what I'm saying is that we both bring our unique skill set into the mix. But what we bring isn't the question. It's what the situation takes away from us."

His brows drew together. "You lost me."

"Can we admit to ourselves if the cons of guardianship outweigh the pros? Or are we too terrified to face the truth? I think that's the issue. You and I are straight shooters. Do the right thing. Are either of us willing to admit that perhaps guardianship might not be the right choice at this time? And can we recognize that saying no doesn't mean we don't love this little girl or her parents?"

He shook his head. "Sadie, the reason I stopped working on the list is because it hurt my heart. I know that Homestead Pass is the best place to raise a child. There's a pro right there. And I also know that I'm not the best choice for guardianship. You are. That's my con."

"What are you saying?"

"I'm saying that maybe you should consider staying in Homestead Pass."

She looked at him. Things had become much too complicated. Staying in Homestead Pass knowing she was becoming attached to a man who held the power to break her heart was a very bad idea. Con. Leaving the college and the possibility of the Manchester Award? Con.

Happily-ever-after was a pro. And it was an illusion. She'd known that all her life.

Drew stood. Was she imagining the sadness in the depths of his blue eyes? He gave her a short salute and turned. "Branding starts tomorrow. So, I'll see you when I see you."

See you when I see you. Would that someday be their parting song?

Sadie pulled out a notebook and opened it up. No matter how painful the outcome, it was time for a heart-to-heart with herself and time to finish her list. She said a silent prayer as she began to write.

Drew sat down on the blanket next to Sadie and picked up a leg of fried chicken from his plate. Around them, the church spring picnic was in full swing. "I'm glad you decided to come today, Sadie."

"So am I."

"Mind if I ask what made you change your mind?"

"Wednesday is Mae's surgery. Who knows what will happen after that? This might be the last time I get to spend with this community."

"Sadie, you're always welcome in Homestead Pass. No one is kicking you out. It's your choice."

"Let's have a moratorium on post-op discussions for today."

"Fine with me. What do you want to talk about?"

"How about that fried chicken you're eating."

Drew wiped his face with a napkin. "Now, that's a topic I am happy to discuss. The pastor's wife makes the best fried chicken. I'm still licking my lips."

"Don't let Bess hear you say that."

"It's okay because Bess makes the best cinnamon rolls."

"Did you try my cookies?" she asked. "They were at the end of the dessert table."

"Brought my own." He pulled a container out of the picnic basket.

"You swiped the ones from the kitchen counter?"

"*Swiped* seems harsh. I figured you set them aside for me." He narrowed his gaze as he stared across the grassy church grounds. "Is that Lucas with Mae?"

"Yes. He offered to give me a break. Wasn't that thoughtful?" She adjusted her dress around her legs and crossed her ankles, revealing sassy red polka-dot flats. Sadie and her shoes.

"Thoughtful?" He laughed. "You do realize that he's using Mae as bait, right?"

Sadie turned to him, alarmed. "Pardon me?"

"Look over there by those picnic tables. See my brother? Luc is using Mae to attract females."

"No." Sadie scoffed. "Your brother wouldn't do that."

Drew began to laugh. "Sadie, you've got a lot to learn about guys."

"If what you say is true, then why aren't you doing the same thing?"

"Because if I have to use a baby to get a gal's attention, she's probably not the gal whose attention I'm interested in.

"I see."

Did she? He could only smile. The truth was that the gal whose attention he sought already had the baby. He longed to tell Sadie how he felt, but every time he tried, something held him back. Maybe it was fear, like Gramps had said.

He gave up and reached for another cookie.

"You made these in cooking class?"

"Yes. Pignoli." She frowned. "Why?"

He eyed the golden-brown cookie with pine nuts before he took a bite and savored the flavor. "I've noticed you're trying your hand at cooking and baking more often."

"Bess is teaching me. I've filled an entire notebook with recipes I have mastered."

Drew nodded. "Mind if I ask you a question?"

"Go ahead."

"Who made lunch for the crew when I was out of town?"

An indignant expression crossed her face, and she primly folded her hands in her lap. "What makes you think I didn't make lunch?"

"Now, don't take offense. You have many talents. However, by your own admission, cooking has not been on your agenda. I believe you mentioned avocado toast as your go-to meal."

She opened her mouth to protest, and he held up a hand.

"Let me finish. These cookies are delicious. I am convinced that you can do anything you set your mind to."

"But? I hear a 'but' in there," she said.

"But you'd only been on the ranch a short time when I left for Billings, and Bess came down with that virus. It's been nagging at me since then. You said you got help from your friends. Sort of cryptic, don't you think?"

"If I tell you, you can't say anything." She glanced around and then met his gaze. "I'm serious, Drew."

"Do you trust me?"

"I do." She leaned close, strands of dark hair providing

a veil between them and the world. "Olivia Moretti," she whispered, her breath warm against his face.

Drew's eyes flew open. "Liv is back in town?"

"No. She was here for her father's birthday and didn't want Sam to know." Sadie played with the edge of the blanket. "Sam and Olivia were engaged, Bess said."

"Yeah. All I know is she left town. I don't ask questions." He offered a resigned smile. "The Morgan men don't have the best track record with women."

"Oh, that's not true. You told me that your parents had a great marriage."

"Not a hereditary condition." If only it were, he wouldn't be living on a ranch with four bachelors.

They were silent for minutes, then Drew turned to Sadie. "Ever think about marriage?"

"Are you asking me if I've ever been married before? Because if you are, the answer is no. However, I have read extensively on the subject of love and marriage."

He raised a brow. "Shakespeare? Aren't those tragedies and comedies?"

"I'm not talking about Shakespeare. I mean my own research."

Drew worked not to laugh. "Tell me you didn't just say that."

She gestured with a raised hand. "Is that a problem?"

"Okay, let's back up a bit, then." He frowned. "What are your thoughts on falling in love?"

"My thoughts?"

"Yeah. Have you done much research?"

"*Love* is an abstract term and I'm a literal thinker."

"Mind if I ask if you've ever been in love?"

"I don't think so." She paused and narrowed her eyes. "Maybe when I was in third grade."

Drew chuckled. "I would have liked to know Sadie Ross in third grade."

"No, you wouldn't have. I was a mess."

"Friends care for each other, even when they're a mess."

She smiled and seemed to see far into the distance. "You're right about that."

"Thinking about Delia?" he asked.

"Yes. She was a good friend."

"So was Jase." Drew sigh, thinking. "We were fortunate to each have a friend like that in our lifetime."

"Yes. You're right." She met his gaze and offered a sad smile. "You do that very well," she said.

"Do what?"

"You turn things around and find the happiness in a situation that's not so happy."

He shrugged. "My father did that. I guess I'm living his legacy."

Across the way, Lucas waved at them. "I better go grab Mae," he said. "My guess is that she needs a diaper change, which has greatly diminished her chick-magnet potential."

"I'll get her. You relax. You've barely had a free minute or a night's sleep this week."

He stood and helped her to her feet. "Thanks, Sadie."

She ran a hand through her dark hair, and he noticed the silver bracelet on her wrist. That made him smile, and for a moment, he watched her walk across the grass toward his brother, savoring the moment. Around him, families enjoyed lunch, and the clang of metal indicated horseshoe games in progress. It occurred to him that life was pretty much perfect right now.

"Got any of those cookies left?"

"Huh?" Drew turned his head to see his grandfather ease into a lawn chair.

"Cookies. You having hearing problems?"

"No, I was thinking." He handed the container over and sat back on the ground, his gaze following Sadie again.

"What were you two talking about with such serious expressions?" Gramps asked.

"Love."

"Love?" His grandfather chuckled. "What do you know about love?"

"Not much."

"Got that right. I think you could fish in a barrel and miss."

"I don't think the situation is that dire, but thanks for the vote of confidence."

Gramps reached for another cookie. "The way I see it, if a man is smart, and does it right the first time, then he only needs one shot. It's okay to mess up, but you gotta learn from your mistakes."

"Is that from some self-help book?" Drew asked.

"No, it's from Gus Morgan's book."

"That's your philosophy on love?" Drew shook his head.

"Pretty much my philosophy on everything."

"When it comes to love, though. Did you learn from your mistakes, Gramps?"

His grandfather scoffed. "Didn't make any mistakes. Fell in love with your grandmother. The end."

"That doesn't make you an expert. It makes you blessed."

"Yeah." He looked at Drew and grinned. "You're probably right."

His grandfather examined a cookie and nodded with approval. "Sadie is turning out to be an excellent baker."

"Uh-huh." Drew leaned to the right so he could see around a group of kids who'd blocked his line of sight to Sadie. She stood laughing with Lucas and his friends. His chest tightened. Sadie was easily the prettiest woman here.

The cowboys talking to her probably realized that as well. Not that he was jealous or anything.

"You know, you're different since Sadie's come to the ranch," his grandfather said.

He turned to see the older man eyeing him, much like he'd inspected the cookie. "Different how?"

"Relaxed. Happy. The two of you are always putting your heads together and talking like you have a secret."

"No secrets, Gramps. Except Mae."

"Did you ask Sadie to stay in Homestead Pass, like I told you?"

"I might have mentioned it a time or two." Drew released a breath. The last thing he wanted to think about today was how Sadie could very well be leaving soon. They were both still avoiding thinking past the surgery. He reached for his water bottle.

"Think she heard you?"

"Hard to say. She's got a lot on her mind. Her career. Her life in Tulsa."

"That so?" He nodded thoughtfully. "If her life in Tulsa is so important, how come she's only been back to check on her life once since she showed up?" He shot Drew a cynical expression. "I don't think it's as important as she remembers."

Drew raised his brows, recalling Sadie's words when she came back from Tulsa. What she wanted was here in Homestead Pass. She'd said that. Even suggested working remote. But was there enough time to pursue such a possibility?

"Maybe all she needs is a good reason to stay."

"She has one. Mae."

His grandfather released a frustrated breath. "No wonder you don't date."

"What are you trying to say?"

"I'm telling you that you need to speak plain. Don't beat round the bush. And don't make staying just another option. Let her know you *want* her to stay. *Need* her to stay."

For a second or two, he just stared at his grandfather. The man was spouting things Drew only dared to think about when he lay down to sleep at night.

"No use denying it," Gramps said. "You may not know a thing about love, but clearly it has you by the tail."

When he opened his mouth in denial, his grandfather shook his head. "Don't even."

"Look, Gramps. You don't get it. I can't tell Sadie to stay. If she stays in Homestead Pass, it has to be because *she* wants to. Not because I want her to."

His grandfather's expression turned impatient. "Did your mother drop you on your head when you were a baby?"

Drew laughed loud and hard and got to his feet. "I'm going to go save Sadie and Mae from those yahoos over there."

"You can run, but you can't hide. The sun is out. The azaleas are blooming. Today would be a good day to ask her to stay."

"Thanks for the advice, Gramps." He strode across the lush grass to his brother's side. Sadie's back was to him as she discussed the finer points of *Macbeth* with a young cowboy in a Stetson too big for his head.

"Line forms to the right," Lucas muttered, nudging Drew out of the way with his elbow.

"You think, little brother."

As if sensing his presence, Sadie turned, and her face lit up. At the response, Drew stepped through the throng of cowboys and took Mae from her arms. "Ready to go home?" he asked, his eyes only on Sadie.

"I am." She smiled at the group. "I enjoyed chatting with you, fellas."

Drew adjusted his hat and shot Lucas a wink.

"Thank you for the rescue," Sadie murmured.

"That's what I'm here for." He grinned. Yep, Gramps was right about one thing. Today was pretty much a perfect day. Now all he had to do was figure out how to make Sadie think so too.

Chapter Ten

Drew closed his eyes and opened them again. "Sadie. You're making me dizzy."

Sadie paced back and forth one more time across the polished gray speckled linoleum before she stopped to face him. "Why hasn't someone come to give us an update?"

He leaned back in the plastic chair of the hospital waiting room and crossed his arms. "That question has been answered already. They'll come out when surgery is over."

She strode to the end of the waiting area and stood looking out the big window at the clear blue Tulsa sky, then she walked back and stood in front of him again. "Do you think they'll let us stay in her room tonight?"

"I already asked. Only one parent can be in the room at a time after visiting hours." He examined the magazines on the table. The latest issues of *Crochet Monthly* and *Opera Journal* did their best to tempt him. He should have brought a book so he could at least pretend he was calm. Instead, he pulled out his phone and checked messages.

"We aren't parents," Sadie said.

"We have medical power of attorney," he reminded her. "That makes us parents."

"Yes. Yes. That's right." She nodded, and he could practically see her brain shooting off neurons a mile a minute.

"I know I'm preaching to the choir here, but things are going to be fine. We're prayed up, and Dr. Bedford has assured us that she's performed this procedure dozens of times."

"I envy both your calm and your confidence." She narrowed her gaze. "What do you think about hiring a nurse for a few days?"

"Whatever you want, but the doc said she didn't think it was necessary the first six times you asked her."

Sadie glared at him, and then her faced crumpled. "I hated seeing her on that hospital bed with those tubes in her arms."

Yeah, he agreed. It nearly killed him when Mae had disappeared through the double doors away from them. They'd made a promise to take care of Delia and Jase's baby. But she was in the Lord's hands now.

Sadie began to worry the floor again. This time, circling the row of chairs, over and over again.

"Sit down for a minute, would you?" he asked. "You've been pacing and talking like a squirrel who's had too much sugar for the last hour. I'm exhausted watching you."

"I don't think I can sit."

"Sure you can." He patted the bright orange plastic chair next to his. "Tell me about you and Delia."

She sank into the chair, the tension going out of her like the air out of a deflated balloon. "This is so not how I expected things to turn out."

"What do you mean?"

"Delia had it all. She was my hero."

"Sadie, did it ever occur to you that you were Delia's hero?" He reached out and took her hand, rubbing his thumb over the soft skin. She had no clue how brave and courageous she was.

"That's a nice thing to say," she murmured.

"It's the truth." He smiled. "How long did you know Delia?"

"Forever. I told you. She saved me. When I was returned to the group home, she found me. She never left me." Sadie looked up at him. "That's why I can't leave Mae. She has to come with me to Tulsa. I promised Delia. In my heart, I promised her."

A lone tear journeyed down Sadie's face. She wiped at it and looked away. "I'm not crying."

"No. Of course not." Drew inhaled. It had to take a lot of work not to cry.

"How about a cup of coffee?" he asked. "I can go down to the cafeteria and get the good stuff."

"Hot chocolate sounds good."

"One hot chocolate coming up." He stood and met her gaze. "I want you to promise me you won't go to the information desk while I'm gone and ask them to check on Mae."

"I only did that once or twice."

"Four times. You asked them four times." As he spoke, the woman at the desk eyed them suspiciously.

"Fine."

Drew got off the elevator at ground level only to find Sadie's boss, Leah, waiting for an up elevator. He recognized her from the video chats with Sadie.

Smartly dressed in black with large bright red beads around her neck and red shoes on her feet, she carried a black leather tote. He would have taken her for a magazine editor instead of a college professor.

"Ms. Telfer." He offered a smile, happy to see any friend

of Sadie's. "You probably don't remember me. I'm Drew Morgan, from Homestead Pass."

"Oh, I remember you. You're Sadie's cowboy." She pulled up her oversize glasses and looked him up and down. A grin lit up her face. "You look even better in person."

"Glad to hear that." He chuckled.

"Sadie is on the sixth floor?"

"Yes, in the waiting area."

"Thank you, Drew." She hesitated. "What do you think about the Manchester Award nomination? I'm sure you're as thrilled as I am for Sadie. It's quite an honor to even be nominated, you know. And if she wins?" Leah grinned. "Who wouldn't want a year in London, right?"

"Right. Of course. And as you said. Quite an honor." He nodded toward the cafeteria. "I'll see you up there. I'm going to grab some coffee."

Manchester Award? Why hadn't Sadie mentioned that? Seemed like a big deal. Did she think he wouldn't understand? Working on a ranch was a far cry from a college campus, but he had gone to college and did occasionally kick the mud off his boots.

The more he thought about what Leah said, the more irritated he became. Instead of going straight back to the waiting area, he sat at a booth, nursed a quick cup of coffee and felt sorry for himself. Drew had half a dozen questions, though he wouldn't say anything today.

He glanced at his watch and stood. No, today was all about Mae.

When he got off the elevator with Sadie's hot chocolate in his hand, the voices of Bess and his grandfather carried down the hall.

"I know you said it wasn't necessary to come, but how could I stay away?" Bess said. "My prayer group met at the house, and they brought casseroles. They're on their knees until we hear our good report."

"Thank you, Bess," Sadie said. "Why casseroles?"

"It's how people show their love," Gramps said. "They cook."

"That's so sweet."

"Yep, pies, too," his grandfather said.

Drew gave Gramps a nod and handed Sadie her hot chocolate.

"How are you doing, Drew?" Bess asked.

"I've had better days." He checked his watch. "The surgery is expected to take two hours, and we're coming up on that now."

"Maybe we should check on things." Sadie glanced at the information desk.

"You're going to get us kicked out of here," Drew said.

Bess put an arm around Sadie. "I don't know who started the tradition of fretting, but it sure has deep roots, doesn't it?"

Sadie nodded and put on a brave smile.

"Truth is, it doesn't move the Lord," Bess continued. "So, let's give Mae over to Him and not take the situation back. I am guessing He can handle it."

"You're right." Sadie sighed. "Of course you're right."

Drew glanced around. "I saw your boss, Leah, downstairs. Isn't she here?"

"She hugged me and left. I thought we could meet and discuss the situation at the college, but I can't think about anything but Mae."

The sound of hydraulic doors opening had everyone turning to see Dr. Bedford appear in blue scrubs with a blue surgical cap hiding her hair. She approached them with a smile. "Dr. Ross, Mr. Morgan?"

"Yes, ma'am," Drew said.

"I'm pleased to say that the procedure was a success," the doctor said. "Not a single issue. Your girl is in recovery, and we expect continued progress."

"Well, praise the Lord." Bess gave a hoot and proclaimed the words loud enough for the entire hospital to hear.

His grandfather punched the air. "I second that."

"What do we do next?" Drew asked.

"Someone will get you when her room is ready."

One night in the hospital. That was all it was. Drew kept reminding himself of that as he shifted position in the plastic chair hours later. He was ready to hunt down the guy who'd invented waiting room chairs. They were torture devices made to encourage leaving, not waiting.

At four in the morning, Drew traded places with Sadie. She went to the waiting room, and he settled into the cushioned and marginally less comfortable version of the waiting room chair right next to Mae's crib. Soft, even breathing told him Mae was asleep, and the constant beep of an IV machine counted down the minutes until dawn.

He hadn't set foot in a hospital since his parents had died. Didn't care to, ever again. Hospitals were a reminder of all he'd lost. Except for tonight. Tonight, they were a mile marker. Maybe the last mile marker before Sadie left. An ache started in his throat and moved to his heart.

Daylight streamed through the window when a cheerful nurse came into the room with a bottle for Mae.

"I can feed her," he said.

"Wonderful." She handed him the bottle. "Just let me know how much she takes."

He nodded.

"We don't get a lot of papa bears spending the night," she said. "Usually, it's the momma bears." She smiled. "Good for you, Dad."

Dad. There it was again. If only he could live up to such a title. He'd worked on his list this last week, and more and more, everything pointed to Sadie taking guardianship. She'd proven she could do the job, probably better than him. More than that, Sadie needed to raise her friend's baby. Mae had become her whole heart. He didn't know if he could take that away from her.

It didn't take long for Mae to eagerly finish the bottle and sit up in the crib, curiously looking around.

"Drew?"

He turned at the sound of Sadie's voice. She looked as rumpled and exhausted as he felt as she approached the crib and stroked Mae's forehead. "Sweet baby," she murmured.

Mae chortled in response.

"She's happy to see you," Drew said.

"I'm happy to see her too." Sadie looked up at him and yawned. "Did you get any rest?"

"Are you kidding? They run a tight ship here. A nurse checked on Mae every two hours. What about you?"

"Not much, but I did see the doctor a few minutes ago. She's working on discharge orders and will be in soon to check her. That's why they let me in here." She frowned, thinking. "Or it could be because they wanted me to stop bothering them."

Drew chuckled and took a deep breath. "Well, Sadie. We made it."

"Yes, we did," she said softly. "That was the longest night of my life. I never want to go through that again." Stepping close, Sadie wrapped her arms around his waist before burying her head against his chest. Shocked, Drew hesitated before he stroked her long hair.

"It's okay," he murmured.

Yeah, it was all going to be okay. The worst was over.

All they had to do was pick a guardian.

So simple, and yet, so complicated.

"You are the best post-op patient in the world," Sadie said. She carried Mae on her hip, dancing down the hall toward the kitchen. The baby laughed with each step. "Only a week, and the doctor says you are one hundred percent cleared for fun."

Mae offered random syllables in response.

"Let's find your bonnet and go for a walk with Cooper and Drew. Would you like that?"

She called out, "Bess, did you happen to see Mae's yellow bonnet?" Sadie brushed golden wisps of hair back from Mae's face as they walked into the kitchen.

"Bess?" Sadie looked up to see the housekeeper sprawled on her back on the kitchen floor. Her stomach dropped.

"Bess!" she managed through the tightening in her chest. At the urgency in her voice, little Mae began to cry. "No, baby girl. Don't cry. It's going to be okay."

Please, God, let it be okay.

Sadie ran back to the nursery and placed Mae in her crib while furiously shoving back her fear. Then she raced to the kitchen and slid to the floor and Bess's side.

"Bess!" This time she called louder and nudged her shoulder. There was no response. The housekeeper's color seemed ashen, her lips slightly blue.

Okay, okay. Think, Sadie.

Calm down and think. You read up on CPR when you arrived at Lazy M.

But you aren't trained, her mind shot back.

I can do this.

Sadie put her fingers on Bess's neck. *That's a pulse. Definitely a pulse.*

She leaned close, her ear to the housekeeper's chest, and listened for breathing.

Bess is breathing. Oh, thank You, God.

"Sadie, are you ready? I've got the stroller." Drew stepped into the kitchen with Cooper trailing behind.

He froze in the doorway. Behind him, Cooper howled.

"Drew, call 9-1-1," Sadie ordered.

His face paled, but he didn't move.

"Drew! Look at me! Drew! Can you hear me?"

"Yeah. Yeah." The words came out in short, painful gasps.

"Call 9-1-1. Take Cooper outside, and then come back and let me know what they say. Tell them we found Bess unresponsive. She's got a weak pulse, and she's breathing. No injuries that I can see."

Eyes fixed on Bess, he still didn't move.

"Go, Drew."

"I'm going."

Sadie continued to monitor Bess's pulse and breathing while silently praying.

"Ooh," Bess moaned, and her lashes fluttered.

"Thank you," Sadie whispered. She pushed Bess's curls from her face. "It's okay, Bess."

"What happened?" she asked weakly.

In the distance, the sound of sirens echoed, getting closer and closer.

Drew came back into the kitchen. The color had returned to his face, and he seemed to be functioning on all cylinders again. "Homestead Pass Fire and Rescue is two minutes out. Ambulance is on the way."

"Can you move your truck and direct them to the house?"

"Got it."

"I need to get up," Bess moaned.

Sadie put a gentle hand on her chest. "No. Stay still. We'll get you checked out, and then you can get up."

"I'm so dizzy. Why am I so dizzy?" Bess mumbled.

"What's going on, Sadie? I hear sirens." Gus stepped into the room. His eyes were wide with shock when he saw her on the floor with Bess. "Is she okay?"

"Bess isn't feeling well. We've called 9-1-1. Gus, will you check on Mae? She's in her crib."

"Yes, ma'am."

A minute later, the room was filled with paramedics and firefighters. So many people crowded into one room. The kitchen no longer seemed to be a kitchen but the stage for a medical drama unfolding.

Once Sadie shared the details of how she'd found Bess, she backed up. She continued to back up, away from the commotion, until she was in the hallway leading to Drew's office and against the wall with her arms tightly hugging her body.

If only she could stop trembling. Her heart pounded in her ears as she reviewed what had happened over and over, on a continuous loop in her mind.

What if she hadn't been here? What if Bess had been alone in the house? What if Bess had been injured? Sadie's stomach lurched at the thought.

She heard Drew's voice but couldn't see him between the wall of first responders. He calmly answered questions about Bess's background and medical history.

The buzz of the voices merged into a drone of white noise as they evaluated Bess. At intervals, the static sound of a two-way radio cut into the conversation. All Sadie could see from her vantage point was an IV bag held in the air, its tubing dangling toward where Bess lay on the floor. It seemed like hours before someone pushed the kitchen table out of the way, and first responders dispersed enough to allow a stretcher into the room.

Then Drew was at her side. "They're transporting her to Elk City."

"Did anyone say what's wrong with her?"

"No. I heard comments about her heart. But nothing I can confirm."

The back door screen banged against the wall as Sam and Trevor raced into the house. "What's going on?" Sam asked.

"Bess collapsed," Sadie said.

"She's on her way to the hospital," Drew added. "Right now, she appears to be stable and alert."

"Bess?" Sam shook his head and grimaced as if in pain. "She's been our rock for nearly twenty years." His deep voice was thick with emotion.

"Anyone know how to reach her sons?" Trevor asked.

"Maybe the pastor does," Drew said. "I'll step into my office and call."

Sam looked around wild-eyed. "Where's Gramps? Is Gramps okay?"

"Right here." Gus strode down the hallway. "I'm just fine." He put a gentle hand on Sadie's arm. "Mae has fallen asleep."

"Thank you," she breathed.

"Look, they're heading out to the ambulance with the stretcher," Trevor said.

Sadie moved closer, hoping for a glimpse of her friend and mentor. "We should go to the hospital. Bess shouldn't be alone."

Sam looked at his brother, and Trevor gave a nod of agreement. "Trev and I will go."

"I'm coming too," Gramps said. "You and Drew have had enough of hospitals of late. I'll call as soon as we know something."

"Thank you, Gus," Sadie said.

"Not a thing to thank me for. It's you two who we oughta be thanking." He shook his head. "That was some quick thinking. You saved Bess's life."

"It was all Sadie," Drew said from behind her.

Sam and Trevor headed out the back door with Gus trailing as the ambulance doors clanged shut and the vehicle started down the drive with lights and sirens.

With the kitchen emptied, Sadie walked through the area, numbly picking up wrappers and debris, evidence of what had happened. In the corner of the room, she found Bess's silver filigree watch. It held no value except sentimental. The paramedics must have removed it from her wrist. Sadie tucked it into her pocket.

She shoved the kitchen table back into place and moved the chairs into their proper position. Bess would want everything in order.

The oven beeped, and Sadie turned, surprised. She donned gloves to open the door and removed a pan of plump and golden cinnamon rolls before turning off the oven.

Bess's rolls. Sadie nearly lost her composure against a wave of emotion.

It only took moments for the sweet scent of cinnamon and orange to fill the kitchen, chasing the last traces of the emergency from the room.

"Hey, I need to apologize."

Sadie turned from the counter to find Drew standing in the doorway with his hands in the pockets of his Wranglers. "Apologize? Why?"

He glanced at her and then away. "I froze back there. Literally froze. I couldn't move."

"You don't need to apologize. We're a team, and we got the job done."

"Yeah, but you don't understand, Sadie. I panicked. I

can and have managed any number of emergencies out there. Births and deaths and everything in between." He waved an arm toward the pasture. "When I saw Bess lying there, not moving… Everything went blank." Anguish filled his eyes. "What if I do that with Mae?"

"You won't." She met his gaze. "Maybe both of us should take some basic first aid and CPR classes."

He seemed to calm down at the words. "Maybe so."

Sadie looked around the room, once again living through the incident. Except this time, all the fear she'd held at bay the last hour came crashing down. Bess had to be okay. Please, Lord, let her be okay.

She sank into a chair.

"Sadie?" Drew knelt in front of the chair.

"Don't ask. I am not fine."

He took her in his arms and held her. The slow, deep sound of his breathing soothed her soul. She could stay here forever. But forever had never been her friend.

"You can cry, you know. I won't tell anyone." His voice rumbled in his chest and against her ear.

"Crying never changes anything," she murmured.

"Oh, Sadie. Who told you such a tall tale?"

From down the hall, Mae began to fuss, and he released her. "I'll get Mae."

Sadie put a hand over her mouth and worked to slow her heart and push back the pummel of emotions. Once again, she murmured prayers for her friend.

In her mind, she saw Bess at the sink, laughing. Saw the pride with which she served up her famous cinnamon rolls. And the conspiratorial whispers as they planned the horse-riding lesson behind Drew's back.

The housekeeper had become not only a friend but a mother.

Sadie couldn't bear to lose her.

Chapter Eleven

"How's Bess today?" Sadie walked into the kitchen from the laundry room at the same time Drew entered from the front hall. She placed an overflowing basket of towels on the kitchen table and began to fold. It was an activity she'd watched Bess do dozens of times over the last weeks.

"Cranky." Drew took off his hat and grabbed a mug from the cupboard. "Although she did have a good word for your cookies."

Sadie smiled at his answer, delighted that Bess had her spunk back again.

"She was cranky yesterday too. Steer clear of talk about the pacemaker or hospital food."

"What was the final diagnosis?" Sadie asked.

"Heart failure. The pacemaker is supposed to correct the problem, along with diet and medications."

"I'm grateful for answered prayer," Sadie said.

"Me too." He lifted the coffee carafe. "This coffee fresh?"

"Not Bess fresh, but it's passable."

Drew filled a mug and sniffed the liquid. "Are you kidding me? This stuff should come with a warning label."

"Your grandfather made it."

"Not surprised. Gramps thinks coffee is weak unless

you can stand a spoon up in it." Drew sat down at the table. "Did I mention that if all her lab work and tests come back clear, Bess will be discharged this afternoon?"

"I know she'll be glad to be in her own bed. Poor Bess. She's used to being in charge." Sadie shook her head. She could well relate. "Is her family still here?"

"Yeah, and she's still got casseroles arriving hourly. Payback for all she's done for folks over the years." Drew slid into a kitchen chair and reached into the basket to help fold towels.

They worked in companionable silence until the basket was empty. Sadie smiled for no good reason, or maybe because she knew she'd always cherish memories of simple things like folding towels in the kitchen with Drew.

He chuckled, and she looked at him. "What?"

"She also threatened to show up on the ranch tomorrow." He slid his pile of kitchen towels across the table to her as he spoke.

"I hope you were able to dissuade her."

"I said that, as her employer, I was required to ask for a cleared-to-work slip from her physician." He smiled. "Who knew that sweet Bess Lowder had such a colorful vocabulary?"

Sadie chuckled. She opened a drawer and carefully tucked some dish towels inside, precisely the way Bess liked them.

"Hey, I've been meaning to congratulate you on your nomination for that award. Big deal, I hear."

She froze and slowly turned around, unnerved by the comment. "You know?"

"Leah told me at the hospital."

"You've known all this time? Why didn't you say something before this?"

He wrapped his hands around his mug and looked at

her as though gauging her reaction. "I think the question is, when were you going to tell me?"

Sadie searched for a response. "It's only a nomination."

The oven buzzed, and she quickly donned oven mitts and pulled the dinner casserole out, relieved by the distraction. "This is Bess's recipe. I hope it's good." She paused. "We were out of cream-of-mushroom soup, so I improvised."

"Sadie, sit down. I don't care about casseroles. When were you going to tell me that you're leaving?"

Surprised at his words, Sadie sat and folded her hands in her lap. She hadn't expected to have this conversation here and now. She'd planned to wait until after dinner when he was relaxed, Mae was asleep and there wasn't a chance of someone walking in.

"I didn't decide until Bess landed in the hospital." She shifted in the chair and ran her fingers over the grain lines in the oak table. "But if I'm honest, I knew it was coming. So did you."

"That's not true. I worked on my list as you asked. Every time I looked at it, I realized you should be Mae's guardian. The incident with Bess only confirmed my conclusion."

Sadie gave a grim shake of her head. "I disagree. My list told me that Mae belongs here with you on Lazy M Ranch, with Gus and Bess and your brothers. There is so much love here for Delia and Jase's child."

He frowned. "What about you, Sadie? You were born to be a mother. I've been in awe of you since day one. There is no challenge you back down from, you're never discouraged, and you're a stubborn advocate for Mae."

"You may be exaggerating. I was a hot mess at the hospital."

"You were perfectly imperfect. Which is exactly what Mae needs."

"Does she?" Sadie prayed for calm as she got her next words out. "There is one thing I cannot provide Mae. Family. Or the Lazy M Ranch. You have more than enough of both."

Drew gripped the mug. "You're giving her up?"

Sadie swallowed. Why did he have to keep pushing? She'd made the decision. The right decision for Mae. Wasn't that enough? Being calm and rational was killing her.

"No. Not at all. I'll be here visiting whenever I can. As long as you'll allow me to."

His jaw tightened, and he gave a slow shake of his head. "I never took you for a quitter."

Annoyance flared, and she tamped it down. He was angry and wanted to argue. The realization helped her calm down. She would state her case and let it go.

"I'm not quitting. I'm making the best choice for Mae." She held her hands together tightly. "Bess's health scare made me realize that we have to stop dragging our feet. That paperwork needs to be signed immediately. I'm waiting for a callback from Mr. Whitaker to let him know."

"You're changing the subject. Mae loves you. How are you rationalizing that in your head? What data do you have to offer for leaving Delia's baby?'

She heard the ache in his voice, and it was almost her undoing. But she had to be strong for Mae.

"I love her too, but she doesn't belong in a cramped apartment when she can have it all here with a grandfather and uncles to dote on her."

Sadie looked out the window at the Oklahoma sky. The same sky as in Tulsa, only miles and miles apart. She'd miss this place every single day.

"What about Cooper? You're going to leave Cooper too?" His voice nearly cracked with the question.

Cooper. The goofy dog lived for an opportunity to

shower her with unconditional affection in exchange for a good rub. Sadie blinked. She would miss Cooper.

Stick to the facts, Sadie.

Your heart has no place in this conversation.

Her breath came out unevenly as she worked to focus. "Drew, I live in a small one-bedroom apartment. I don't have room for a dog right now. Even if I get a house, I'd be at the college most of the time. Neither Mae nor Cooper deserves that."

"What about working remote?" he asked. "You sounded encouraged about that possibility."

"Finding a remote job takes time. Time is the one thing we don't have."

"I guess when you get that award, you'll be spending a year in London," he mused. "Sounds like the perfect place for the woman with a degree in Shakespearean studies to land. Three hundred museums. That has Sadie written all over it."

She blinked, surprised at the comment. "How do you know about the museums?"

"Apparently, you're rubbing off on me. I pulled a Sadie and researched it. Very prestigious award. I'm happy for you."

"There are no guarantees. These things can be political, and I haven't been much of a brownnoser. I don't have high expectations."

"Sadie, you have zero expectations. That's the problem."

"Excuse me?"

"Zero expectations. You won't even fight for what you want. You expect to be rejected."

"That's not true," she huffed, outraged at the comment. She was a fighter. That was how she'd survived her childhood.

"Sadly, it is." He took a deep breath. "So now we have a plan. How is this going to play out?"

Without complications.

"We'll want to give you a little going-away party."

"No." The word fairly burst from her lips. "I don't do goodbyes. I've spent my life saying goodbye. If you have no objections, I'm going to go to Delia and Jase's house tonight. I'll leave the key with Mr. Whitaker."

"Tonight?" He jerked back. "You're leaving tonight? Bess isn't even here."

"I'll call her."

"And slip out of town, like a thief in the night."

"Now you're being dramatic."

"Am I?" He stared right through her with cold, unreadable eyes.

The silence between them was as thick as the Oklahoma humidity.

"I need to check on Mae." Sadie stood and white-knuckled the back of the chair.

"Sure. Um, I won't be here for dinner. I've got someplace to be. I'll let Gramps know. He'll keep an eye on the baby."

"Drew, I want you to know how much I appreciate how you have welcomed me into your home and supported me. You're a good friend and you're going to be a good father to Mae. You're everything Delia and Jase's baby needs."

"That's it?" He gave a slow shake of his head. "That's all?"

"I don't know what you want me to say." *Please, Drew,* she silently begged. *Don't make this harder than it already is.*

He stood and walked out of the kitchen without looking back.

For minutes, Sadie stared at the doorway, unable to move. Then she rushed down the hall toward the nursery.

Mae's latest trick was to toss her toys onto the floor, and several were scattered around the room. Sadie picked up a plush bunny and held it tightly. The soft toy smelled like Mae. She'd never realized babies had their own sweet perfume until now. She was going to miss Mae, just like she missed Delia.

You're doing the right thing. The words echoed over and over.

Tonight should have been easy. Pack her bags, say thank you and walk out the door. She'd done it many times. Only this time, she'd made the mistake of falling in love and forgetting that she was just a temporary member of the family.

"Ma. Ma," Mae babbled.

Sadie's head jerked up. She laughed, buoyed by the simple syllables. She knew the words had nothing to do with her. All the baby books said that first words were often simple, random consonant and vowel combos. Yet, Sadie found herself looking around the room. She longed to yell, holler and let someone know. But Drew was gone, and there was no one to share the precious milestone with.

"Delia," she said aloud. "She's calling you."

Mae sat in the crib, rocking back and forth, gurgling with laughter.

Yes, sweet baby, laugh. Sadie laughed too. She laughed because she'd made the mistake of falling in love with a cowboy who could never be hers. Drew was wrong. For the first time since she was a child in foster care, she had expectations. That was her first mistake.

Sadie glanced at her watch. There were a few hours left with Mae. She scooped the baby up from the crib and headed to the guest room.

"Lord, give me the strength to pack my things up and leave everything I've ever wanted."

Drew stared at the dry-erase board. He shook his head. Sadie and her schedules. Go figure. What used to annoy him would now haunt him for the rest of his life.

Cooper whined at the back door. Drew trudged over and let him in.

"Why aren't you in your crate?"

The dog whined.

"Missing Sadie too? What are we going to do, boy? She left us high and dry."

The dog gave a long, soulful howl.

His grandfather walked into the kitchen. "Cooper spends more time in this kitchen than you do." He opened the refrigerator door and pulled out a pie. "That was mighty good casserole that Sadie made. Did you try some?"

"No, I'm not hungry."

Gus cut a generous slice of pie and walked to the coffee-pot. He narrowed his gaze. "Who made this bathwater?"

Drew glared at him. "We're going to have to come to some sort of compromise on that coffee. I can't drink your gut burner."

"You're mad." His grandfather nodded. "Glad to hear it. Mad means you're still in the game. I'd be concerned if you weren't mad."

"I'm not mad."

"Not mad and not hungry. All good."

"Why is it you're so chipper?" Drew asked. "Don't you miss, Sadie?"

His grandfather held up one finger. "First, Sadie isn't gone. She's right up the road. Told me so herself when she left this afternoon." He held up a second finger. "Second, I'm smart enough to realize this story isn't over."

"Sure it is. She's gone."

"It's kinda like the Bible, son. I know how it ends."

Drew stared at him without saying a word. He didn't know what to say. It seemed he was the only one who realized his life was falling apart around him.

Frustrated, he opened the cupboard, found the dog treats and tossed a few into the hall. The collie barked and raced from the room to retrieve them, skidding across the slick floor into the wall.

Gramps clucked his tongue. "Bess is gonna have a fit if Cooper scratches up that floor."

"She will not. Bess loves Cooper."

The wall clock ticked with a vengeance as Drew tried to figure out how to put one foot in front of the other. He wasn't sure he could stay in the big house any longer. Everywhere he looked, he saw Sadie. Maybe Trevor had an extra bed.

"Do you want some advice?" his grandfather asked.

"Nope." And if he had a brain in his head, he'd get out to the barn and shovel manure. Nothing like hard work to make a fella forget his trouble.

"I'm gonna give it to you anyhow." His grandfather leaned against the refrigerator. "You've been feeling sorry for yourself for hours now, and I'm tired of looking at your pitiful face. May as well sit yourself down."

"This is why people don't ask for your advice."

"I said sit."

Drew sat and tried to remember that he was forty years old and grown men didn't roll their eyes.

"Here's how I see things." Gramps took a deep breath, like a pastor about to deliver a sermon. "You don't want Sadie to leave, and she doesn't want to leave. But the two of you knuckleheads lack the courage to tell each other the truth."

"The truth is, Sadie is gone, Gramps. It's time for things to get back to normal around here."

"You keep saying she's gone. But that's a load of cow paddies." He crossed his arms. "By the way, *normal* has never lived in this house."

Drew met his grandfather's gaze, and something snapped. He released the breath he'd been holding for hours. "I don't know how to change this situation. I can't offer Sadie anything but a house and one-fourth of a ranch in the middle of nowhere."

"Sadie's never had a house."

"She's up for a big award that comes with a year in London. I can't compete with that."

"This isn't a competition. She already chose you."

"I think you're wrong."

"Maybe you should think a little less. Go and talk to her."

"She knows how I feel." Hadn't he told her by the million little things he'd done since he'd figured it out?

"Men and women don't speak the same language naturally." Gramps paced the kitchen with a scowl on his face. "Did you ask her to stay?"

"Not in so many words."

"I don't know how to make this any clearer, son. You have to spell it out. Simple as that. Tell her that you love her."

Drew blinked. He cared about Sadie and longed to hold her and erase her pain. His heart ached with the thought of her leaving. Was that love?

"Oh, good gravy. Are you telling me you haven't figured out you love her until now?"

"I haven't used the words, I guess." He'd never in his life said those words to a woman. Words were a dime a dozen. Action was what counted.

"Good thing you only talk to cattle, or we'd be in a lot of trouble around here."

"There's no need to be insulting." Drew pushed out of the chair and stomped across the kitchen. He opened the cupboard and grabbed a mug. The handle came off in his hands.

For a minute, he just stared at the piece of porcelain.

"Aw, that's an easy fix," his grandfather said.

An easy fix. If only his broken heart was an easy fix.

"Go talk to Sadie and use your words. I promise you. They work. Women need words."

"I'll talk to her in the morning."

"You best catch her before she leaves. And then you be sure to let me know if I'm right or I'm right."

Drew gave up on the coffee and headed to the nursery. "I'm going to look in on Mae."

Gramps nodded. "I'm glad we had this talk."

The night-light lent a soft glow to the nursery and just enough illumination for Drew to see Mae on her back with a hand on her chest.

"Oh, Mae," he whispered. "I'm trying as hard as I can, but she's gone. It's just you and me now."

Mae's lashes fluttered, and she rolled over in the crib. Her head bobbed, and the big blue eyes met his in the dark. She smiled.

"I love you, baby girl."

Mae cooed in response and looked around. Was she looking for Sadie too?

Drew shook his head. "Okay, Gramps," he muttered. "You win."

Maybe she would shut him down, but for Mae's sake, he was going to visit Sadie in the morning. Yep, he planned to be on her doorstep bright and early fighting for what he wanted.

Chapter Twelve

"Maybe this wasn't such a good idea." Sadie sat at the table in Delia's kitchen and nursed a mug of hot tea. Memories of Drew showing her how to warm a baby bottle filled the empty room. He'd been so annoying with his baby-bottle confidence. She could hardly believe at the time that it was her misfortune to be stuck in a house in Homestead Pass with a guy who openly laughed at her analytics.

Then she thought about the good things. How he'd almost kissed her at the stream, and the peonies he'd bought her. She touched the bracelet on her wrist.

She'd been away from Mae and Drew less than eight hours, and already she was in pain. The worst pain of her life. It was different than losing Delia and Jase. There was closure there, knowing her friends were with the Lord. This pain was different. This pain would follow her for the rest of her life because it would be laced with bitter regret.

She could stay in Homestead Pass. But she couldn't make Drew Morgan love her. And even if he wanted her to stay, how long would that last? She'd stick around until one day he decided that, like everyone else, he no longer wanted her.

That made her only option to go back to the hollow life she had in Tulsa.

The front doorbell buzzed, and Sadie glanced at the clock. No one knew she was here except Drew and Gus. Could it possibly be Drew?

Sadie opened the door to find Bess on the porch. She opened the storm door.

"Bess!"

The woman's eyes were warm as she said, "Oh, honey, did you think you could leave town without me tracking you down?"

"How did you know I was here?"

"Gus, of course. And they say women have loose lips."

"Are you supposed to be out and about, Bess?"

"Who's going to stop me?" She moved into the house with a grin and shoved a covered dish into Sadie's arms.

"Did you drive here?" Sadie looked outside, where Bess's pickup truck was parked.

"No. My son hid my keys, so I made him drive me here."

"Do you want to invite him in?"

"No need. You and I are going to chat. He can wait in the car. That's what bossy chauffeurs do."

Bess walked around the living room. "This place looks like a magazine." She smiled. "Are you saying your last farewells to your friends?"

"Yes." She stared at the pictures on the wall, willing herself not to cry. *This. This is why I don't do goodbyes.*

"Hard, isn't it?" Bess offered a cluck of her tongue. "I know goodbye isn't your thing, but you'll have to make an exception for me." She waved a hand. "Kitchen is through there? Let's sit a spell.'

Sadie placed the dish Bess had brought on the counter. "Would you like some tea?"

"No, thank you." She sighed, long and hard. "That cardiologist had the nerve to tell me I can no longer have caffeine. Unless you have decaf, water will be my beverage of choice."

"Water it is." She went to the refrigerator, pulled out a cold bottle of water and removed the lid. "Here you go."

"Thank you." Bess raised her arm, took a sip and grimaced.

"Are you in pain?"

"Just a bit. The sutures around this pacemaker pull if I lift my arm too high. I'm now a bionic woman." She huffed with disgust. "And did I mention the dietician told me I can't make my famous cinnamon rolls anymore." Bess paused. "Okay, to be fair, that's not exactly what she said, but she may as well have."

"Oh, Bess. I'm so sorry." Sadie sank into the chair next to her friend.

"And the icing on the cake? Gus calls me to let me know that my sweet Sadie is leaving." Bess's eyes suddenly overflowed with moisture. She dug in her purse, pulled out a hankie and dabbed at her eyes.

At the sight, Sadie swallowed, blinking back her own tears.

"You have a career in Tulsa that makes you happy. A life there. I completely get that. You're smart, and I imagine that college wants you back pronto." She leaned across the table and took Sadie's hands. "But I have no shame. I don't want you to leave. Period."

When Sadie opened her mouth to answer, Bess shook her head.

"Let me speak my piece while I still have the gumption." She took a breath. "I know you have to, and you're going to, but I won't let you do it without telling you that I love you." She shrugged. "I don't think I'm exaggerating when I say that the Morgan family loves you as well. You belong here."

"Bess." Sadie shook her head and silently pleaded with her not to continue. Staying wasn't an option.

"Don't 'Bess' me. You fit in like you were born to be a Morgan. Think about that, would you?" A sad smile touched her lips. "You're like a daughter to me, and I wouldn't be a very good momma if I didn't tell you that."

"Thank you, Bess." She swallowed and bit her lip, fighting tears. "I love you too."

Bess nodded. "Now, I better get going and leave you to do what you have to do." She stood and glanced around the kitchen. "Oh, that covered dish I brought has fried chicken and mashed potatoes from the pastor's wife. The dietician says I can't eat that either."

Sadie walked Bess to the door, where she was engulfed in a bear hug.

"Bye, bye, sugar."

Sadie waved as the truck backed out of the drive. Then she walked through the empty house, looking at pictures of her friends and remembering the good times, tucking them away in her heart.

In the living room, she sank into a plush chair, pulled out her phone, and began to slide through pictures of Drew, Mae, Gramps, and the rest of the family.

A bubble of pain lodged in her throat, and tears saw the opportunity to slip past her defenses.

Once they began, they wouldn't stop. Sadie cried over all the things she had never cried over.

When she thought she was done, tears flowed again, because she loved Drew and Mae and didn't have a clue how she was going to live without them.

Drew stood outside Delia and Jase's house and stared at the door for a moment. The weather had decided that this was the day to be disagreeable, and at ten o'clock in the morning, it was already humid and ugly and threatening to rain.

He climbed the front steps, his hand resting on the smooth railing once he got to the porch. It seemed he didn't have the energy or the courage to lift his knuckles to the door. Tiredness washed over him in waves, seeping into his body and his soul. He couldn't remember the last time he'd had a good night's sleep. All he did was toss and turn and think until the sun rose.

But thinking had gotten him nowhere.

So, here he was, taking advice from his grandfather. What a sorry state of affairs.

Sadie's car was in the drive, which meant she was still here. That was good, because it had taken forever to hunt down flowers.

This was it. One last try for Mae. Afterward, he'd go back to the Lazy M Ranch, tell his grandfather he was wrong and do his best to move on.

Standing straight, he knocked on the door. It swung open faster than he'd expected, and Sadie stared at him, surprise running wild across her face.

Why did she look so good? His chest ached just gazing at her. Her hair tumbled around her shoulders the way he liked, and she wore a pretty flowered dress and pink flats. She sure had changed since she'd first arrived in Homestead Pass.

The lock clicked as she opened the storm door. "Is something wrong with Mae?"

"No. Something is wrong with me."

"What?" Alarm filled her brown eyes. "Drew, what's wrong?"

He handed her the outrageously huge bouquet of peonies. He'd driven to Elk City for the flowers and bought out the florist. If he was going to be shot down, he wanted to be able to think back and know he'd given it his all.

"Peonies." Her eyes rounded. "Lots of peonies."

"Good fortune, you said."

"I'm confused. You said something was wrong with you."

"Yeah, I've been a fool."

"It's ten a.m. I'm packed to leave town, and you're on the doorstep telling me you're a fool." Sadie cocked her head. "That doesn't strike you as a bit odd?"

"I haven't said the other part."

"What other part?"

"I love you."

For a moment, she stared at him, clearly stunned. Then she shook her head as if to clear her thoughts. "No. No, you don't. You're such a great guy." Her voice was gentle. Like she was stilling a horse. "You always do the right thing, like rescuing dogs. But I'm not one of your strays."

"May I come in? It's stickier than cotton candy out here."

"Sure." She held the door open for him.

He stepped into the foyer and around her suitcase. *All packed and ready to go.* A slow mad began to stir in his gut. There was no way he was going to let her walk away without finally telling her how he felt.

"Let me put these flowers in the kitchen sink."

He followed her into the kitchen. More memories here too. He couldn't escape them.

"When are you leaving?" he asked.

"Soon. Very soon."

"Can you give me a minute to plead my case?"

"Drew—"

He held up a hand. "I'm running out of time. A simple yes or no works. Let me tell you what I came here to say, and then you can walk away." His voice cracked, betraying him. "Forever."

She stilled. "Okay. Yes."

This was going to be awkward. Gramps hadn't given him a word of advice on how he should navigate convincing her to stay.

He'd declared his love.

It hadn't worked.

Fine. He'd do awkward if it meant Sadie would stay.

"I, um…" He swallowed. "We talked about love before, Sadie. At the picnic. Remember?"

She nodded, her face pinched with worry.

"What I didn't say then is that I am forty years old, and I have never told a woman I love her. I've been afraid." He hesitated and then forged on. "I'm not afraid anymore. I love you enough that if you are intent upon leaving, Mae and I will have to move to Tulsa."

"What?" Her head snapped up. "You can't do that. What about the ranch?"

"I talked to my brothers last night, and we're going to restructure the ranch positions."

"What does that mean?"

"It means I no longer want to be in charge twenty-four seven. I've done it for nearly twenty years. I want a life. I want a family." He paused and met her gaze.

She was listening. Listening hard.

"I love you. I need you and Mae to make that happen."

"What happens when you get tired of me?"

He blinked. "Sadie, I'm not going to return you if that's what you think. 'I love you' is forever."

"Forever." Sadie sighed, but he couldn't tell if she was happy or sad.

"Are you okay?" he asked.

"Drew, I know I can make it on my own. I've done it all my life. I am a strong woman. But what this strong woman wants is a family to come home to."

"You do?" Did he dare to hope that maybe she cared?

"Yes. I don't want you to move to Tulsa. I want to stay

in Homestead Pass. I want to live on the ranch with the cows… I mean cattle, and the horses and Mae and you."

"You aren't messing with me?"

She shook her head. "I'm not messing with you."

"What about the award? Will you lose the opportunity?"

"Yes. But I don't care. It's an award. You put it on your desk, and it collects dust. It's not the same as a family. A family is forever."

"And your career?" he asked.

"We'll figure it out as we go."

"What about London?" He didn't want any regrets. Everything needed to be spelled out. Ten years from now, he didn't want to feel like Sadie had missed out on something because of him.

"I can go to London anytime." She shrugged and looked at him. "Maybe *we* can go to London. Together."

At the words, he began to really hope. "Sure, as long as when we're done touring all three hundred museums, we come back to Homestead Pass."

"Yes," she breathed.

"Do you believe that I love you?" he asked. "Forever."

"I do now." She grinned.

He pushed back the brim of his hat and cocked his head. "It's customary to return the sentiment."

Sadie jerked with surprise. "Oh, I'm sorry. I've loved you for weeks."

"You love me." His heart pounded as he repeated the words.

"Drew Morgan, I love you."

He pulled her into his arms and inclined his head. "I've been waiting for this kiss for a long time."

"Me too." She met him halfway and held on tight.

Epilogue

The sound of staple guns and the pounding of hammers filled the spring air. Sadie put on her hard hat and walked through the unfinished house, in search of her husband. It was early afternoon, and she hadn't seen him all day.

She found him in the nursery, on a ladder, measuring the ceiling.

"What are you doing?" she asked.

"I'm thinking a skylight. Right here. Wouldn't it be nice if little Andrew Scott Morgan Jr. could see the sky when he lies in his crib?"

"A wonderful idea." She put a protective hand over her abdomen. "But if you keep making changes to the blueprints, this house will never be completed in time for his birth."

"Point well taken."

She smiled, looking at her cowboy. Was it right to be this happy?

"How are you feeling?" he asked.

"A little tired. I taught that online class this morning, and then Bess and I went to the farmers' market."

"I'll give Mae her bath tonight."

"That would be lovely. Thanks." She reached into her pocket. "Look at this, Helen sent us a card."

"What's it say?" Drew asked. "She doing okay?"

"Better. She likes the extended care facility, and as soon as she's settled we can plan a visit." Sadie smiled. "I'd like to do that before the baby arrives."

"We'll do it. Mae needs grandma time too. In the meantime, I have something to show you." He took her hand and led her through the house to the primary bedroom. "The French doors and balcony are done."

He opened the doors and stepped outside, and she followed. Sadie placed her hands on the railing and inhaled the April air, ripe with the scent of wildflowers. Overhead, the cloudless blue sky seemed to stretch forever. In the distance, the gurgle of water added to the spring melody of chirping birds.

"I can hear the stream," she said.

"Yeah. That is the sound of all my dreams coming true." Drew took her left hand and kissed her ring finger. "One year. Time sure flies, doesn't it? And not a single day goes by that Gramps doesn't say 'I told you so.'"

Sadie nearly snorted with laughter.

"Do you regret that we didn't do a big wedding?" he asked.

"No. I got to visit three hundred museums in London instead."

"There is that." He grinned. "Step over here and check out this view."

She complied, and Drew wrapped his arms around her waist. "Look straight ahead. You can see the big house."

She laughed. "You were right." Then she frowned. "Why are there balloons tied to the front porch?"

"Oh, that."

Sadie turned. "A surprise birthday party, Drew? I thought I made it clear I don't like surprises."

"You were outvoted."

Sadie glanced at her watch. "We have to go pick up Mae from her playdate."

"Okay, but when we get back to the house, act surprised. Bess and Gramps have been working on this for a week."

"You know I will."

"Oh, wait a minute," he said. "I have something for you."

"Drew, you're spoiling me. Peonies were delivered today."

"That's my job." He pulled a small velvet pouch from his pocket. "I didn't have time to wrap it."

She looked from the pouch to him.

"Open it," he said.

She pulled open the drawstring and found a silver chain with a heart-shaped locket. Fingers trembling, she opened the heart. Inside was a picture of Delia on one side and Mae on the other. Tears snuck up on her, falling faster than she could swipe them away. "It's beautiful," she breathed.

Drew removed her hard hat and took the necklace from her fingers. "Turn around." He put the chain around her neck and fastened the catch.

Sadie drew the locket from her chest and opened it once more. She kissed the pictures.

Ah, Delia, my friend. I miss you so.

Then she leaned into her husband's arms and kissed him. Long and slow.

"I love you," she whispered.

"I loved you first," he whispered back.

"No. I actually loved you two weeks before you loved me."

Drew pressed his forehead to Sadie's. "And I imagine you have the data to prove it."

She laughed and put her arms around his neck.

"I do."

* * * * *

Dear Reader,

The Morgan boys of Lazy M Ranch came to life when I received a sweet note card from a friend with a photograph of six cowboys in silhouette standing together, looking out at their spread.

At that moment, Gus, Drew, Sam, Trevor, Lucas and one more cowboy you haven't met were birthed. Sadie Ross walked onto the pages of book one shortly after.

Sadie Ross and Drew Morgan are like peanut butter and jelly. They have nothing in common, but together they create something extraordinary. Each of their weaknesses and strengths complement each other.

Sadie found her forever family and the love of a lifetime, and Drew was able to put aside his fears and finally share all the love he had inside. They are now partners in the good times and the tough times.

I hope you enjoyed Sadie and Drew's story as well as all the wonderful people who have filled their lives. You can learn more about the fictional town of Homestead Pass, Oklahoma, and find several recipes from the book on my webpage, www.tinaradcliffe.com.

Thank you so much for picking up this book, and I pray you have been blessed by this story of unconditional love and God's goodness.

Tina Radcliffe

COMING NEXT MONTH FROM
Love Inspired

HIS FORGOTTEN AMISH LOVE
by Rebecca Kertz
Two years ago, David Troyer asked to court Fannie Miller...then disappeared without a trace. Suddenly he's back with no memory of her, and she's tasked with catering his family reunion. Where has he been and why has he forgotten her? Will her heart be broken all over again?

THE AMISH SPINSTER'S DILEMMA
by Jocelyn McClay
When a mysterious *Englisch* granddaughter is dropped into widower Thomas Reihl's life, he turns to neighbor Emma Beiler for help. The lonely spinster bonds with the young girl and helps Thomas teach her their Amish ways. Can they both convince Thomas that he needs to start living—and loving—again?

A FRIEND TO TRUST
K-9 Companions • by Lee Tobin McClain
Working at a summer camp isn't easy for Pastor Nate Fisher. Especially since he's sharing the director job with standoffish Hayley Harris. But when Nate learns a secret about one of their campers that affects Hayley, he'll have to decide if their growing connection can withstand the truth.

THE COWBOY'S LITTLE SECRET
Wyoming Ranchers • by Jill Kemerer
Struggling cattle rancher Austin Watkins can't believe his son's nanny is quitting. Cassie Berber wants to pursue her dreams in the big city—even though she cares for the infant and his dad. Can Austin convince her to stay and build a home with them in Wyoming?

LOVING THE RANCHER'S CHILDREN
Hope Crossing • by Mindy Obenhaus
Widower Jake Walker needs a nanny for his kids. But with limited options in their small town, he turns to former friend Alli Krenek. Alli doesn't want anything to do with the single dad, but when she finds herself falling for his children, she'll try to overcome their past and see what the future holds...

HIS SWEET SURPRISE
by Angie Dicken
Returning to his family's orchard, Lance Hudson is seeking a fresh start. He never expects to be working alongside his first love, single mom Piper Gray. When Piper reveals she's the mother of a child he never knew about, Lance must decide if he'll step up and be the man she needs.

LICNM0423

HARLEQUIN
PLUS

Try the best multimedia
subscription service for romance
readers like you!

Read, Watch and Play.

Experience the easiest way to get
the romance content you crave.

Start your **FREE TRIAL** at
<u>www.harlequinplus.com/freetrial</u>.